AH, GRACE!

Part three of the trilogy: based on

The Farmhouse on Cemetery Hill RD

and

The Portal

Judith, this cover has changed to a bloody hand emerging from a gravestone. And immediately sales went up. I hope you will enjoy it without the sensational cover. Many thanks Cynthia Herbert-Bruschi Adams

CYNTHIA HERBERT-BRUSCHI ADAMS

ISBN: 978-1-64184-683-7 (Paperback)
ISBN: 978-1-64184-684-4 (Ebook)

DEDICATION

To Roger Andrew Adams for a lifetime of support and love.

ACKNOWLEDGEMENTS

First, I thank Ann Aulerich, not because of alphabetical order but because time after time she extended support to the success of this manuscript by her careful editing, knowledge of punctuation and personal support. If there are errors they certainly belong to me for missing something she said. Roger Adams, as he always does, read each word and gave critical feedback so that the reader should not be confused or the writer disgraced. He and Ann supported this effort each day.

Sarah Torcellini is my technical support and developed/revised our new user friendly website: getbooksbycindy.com. and will support the blog linked to **AH, Grace!** and the books which shall follow. Sally Fraley, MS serves as my research assistant on this and several projects.

An anonymous physician from Hartford Healthcare informed some of the nonfiction medical information although a fair amount remains pure fiction.

And my core of brilliant readers once again provided most valuable feedback so that the completed manuscript would not confuse the reader: Edith Posselt, Ed.D., a well read psychologist; Sharon Cormier, an author herself and a person with a high emotional IQ; and W. Hagan, an author from Southern California who now writes fulltime and provides invaluable suggestions and support.

THANK YOU ALL!

CONTENTS

PROLOGUE

If you have not read **The Farmhouse on Cemetery Hill Rd.** or **The Portal** in recent weeks please let me remind you of some relevant points for understanding what you are about to read in **AH, GRACE!** First, Elena Maria and Matthew Nelson are a young couple who purchase a wonderful antique house near the University of Connecticut where he is a faculty member, and Elena Maria is devoted to restoration and history. She unearths, literally and figuratively, some horrors associated with their house, and several incidents occur that frighten them. One involves Giant Goliath Spiders which inexplicably live in their cellar. They also are plagued by a man living in the woods on the back acres of their property and must deal with at least two bodies buried in the dirt part of their cellar. These bodies are not quietly sleeping and one wishes harm to all who live there.

They fight to conquer the unexpected demons in their home. In so doing, Elena Maria finds the diary of a woman named Emily who owned their home over two hundred years before them. Her story is fascinating leading to complications for those who follow behind. Among these twists is her wish to be buried in their cellar beside the body of her dear adopted son, Will, who is already buried there. He died as the result of bites from the Giant Spiders, BUT this may guarantee he will periodically return to life after a period of dormancy. Emily wants to return to life with him.

Among those who disregard Emily's wishes for her death and burial is a skeletal body in that cellar, of a widow who is so angry she wishes harm to all. Many things occur explaining her anger and history but in the end **The Farmhouse** concludes with her actions costing the life of Elena Maria's mother, who is referred to as "nonna".

Also in this first book, Elena Maria has purchased a handsome old painting of a Civil War captain which will continue to influence their lives as it is he, in this portrait, which represents **The Portal** in book two.

The Portal begins just after the Civil War has ended. The captain in the portrait has been a casualty of the war and his picture ends up hanging on the wall where his widow, Victoria, who is newly remarried to the Captain's younger brother, Teddy, are living. Teddy has been a good step-grandson to Emily from the first book and is trying to honor her wishes for her burial which occurs as this book begins. Further, Teddy and Victoria are a well meaning couple trying to do right by their neighbors and, with support from their church, are also helping to sponsor a family of emancipated slaves. They even donate land to assist families whose wells seem to have been contaminated by arsenic used in the embalming of the Civil War soldiers who are buried close-by.

Problems arise when the portrait sees his wife day after day living with his brother. His biggest regret has been leaving her too soon and one night, while she thinks she is dreaming, he has stepped-out of the portrait, traveling through the portal it represents, and makes passionate love to her on the parlor floor as though a flesh and blood man. Victoria's current husband discovers this and hates to deny a moment's pleasure to his Civil War hero brother, but his relationship with Victoria becomes complicated when a short time later she is with child and he knows he is not the father. The baby is born under very challenging circumstances, and they name her Grace.

By her tenth year, Grace has caused so much misery for her mother, and for Teddy who is trying to act as her father, that they turn to the portrait for help. As her 'true' dad, and as he sees she is capable of murdering one of Teddy and Victoria's other children, **The Portal**/portrait, breaks her neck and takes her away to live in a state of limbo neither alive nor truly dead.

In part two of **The Portal** we have returned to modern times and Elena Maria is seeking contact with **The Portal** to plead for his help in bringing nonna back from death. Eventually **The Portal** agrees to bring nonna back, but Elena Maria must promise to do him a favor. She promises "anything" to get her mother back. The portrait wants to resurrect Grace and have Elena Maria and Matthew Nelson raise Grace as their daughter. The agreement is reached, and nonna returns to her family. However, Grace's return is not as smooth as she rekindles a relationship with creatures in the basement of the Nelson house, is harmful to the pets, Scruffy the dog, and Sibyl the cat, and eventually attempts to harm the new baby named Mattie by allowing the Giant Goliath Spiders to bite him. Grace's friendship with Emily and Will (who were skeletons in the basement and caretakers of the spiders) leads her into more trouble.

Baby Mattie is saved, but Grace, once again, must be removed by her father from this life. Before **The Portal** kills her this time she allows the spiders to bite her wrists as Emily and Will convince Grace that to die by spider bites is to simply pass into a temporary dormancy: This is how they are managing a half-life half-death existence.

At the end of **The Portal** Grace has been left in the cemetery on the top of Cemetery Hill Road which is a short distance from the home Elena Maria and Matthew own. She has had a funeral and been buried. But the night following her burial the remaining Giant Goliath Arachnids march up the street in the dark and with just the light of the moon. They unearth Grace and begin to pull her body down the hill in her casket as it rests on pine boughs that they are dragging; their silhouettes are visible in the moonlight.

Then **AH, GRACE!** begins…

1

DARKNESS

She awoke as though having been hit by lightening. She took in a huge gasping breath struggling for air. She was engulfed in total darkness; not a crack lined by light, not a pinhole of a glimmer, not even dancing dust particles. She blinked, squeezed her eyes shut and waited, thinking her pupils would adjust to this lack of light, that she would eventually be able to sense something - a white lamp shade, a white bit of a sheet, a light-colored ceiling, but still nothing, only darkness loomed around her. She was so tired, and this staring into the black made her even sleepier. She closed her eyes knowing she must rest, slipping back into a deep sleep.

Later, although she had no sense of how much time had passed, she again awoke; again becoming conscious with a start, but not quite as shocking as it had been. Breathing remained a challenge and the lack of light was unchanged, yet she reasoned surely it must be past dawn, but nothing, blackness was infinity, the absence of light. The only new sensation was a familiar, but unidentifiable odor.

That is when she tried to move, to push first one arm and then the other out away from her body. She tried to move her legs from side to side or even to cross them, but nothing. She could not raise her head nor bend her elbows. She was totally and tightly wrapped. Initially the only thing she could move was her diaphragm as she gulped for air, and was not able to move it much. Then what seemed to be fully in her control was her mouth. She opened it wide, she tentatively cleared her throat, and then she screamed. She screamed with all the energy, air and might that space would allow. She screamed hoping that someone would come to her rescue; open a door, turn on a light, lift a curtain and unbind her.

When nothing happened, and she could scream no more, she fell back into a deep sleep thinking perhaps she had been kidnapped.

She did not remember offering her wrists to the spiders, or the funeral, or all that followed. She did not recall the tears and words of grief that had been spoken, or the prayers sounding like relief coming from her adoptive parents. She didn't recall Emily and Will promising that they would all be together again in the future.

This time, as she lay sleeping, she was awakened by sounds then motion. There was a scraping along both the top of her room and its sides. It continued for some time before the entire room began to shake and she experienced the sensation of rising up. Yes, that was it; she was being lifted but not touched. She must be in a container of some type, and the entire box was being taken up and then out. Then it came to her. She was in a coffin and had been in the ground. The smell she had noticed was that of earth, moist dark dirt below the grass. The wrap in which she was enfolded was a shroud. Grace realized she must be dead and someone was moving her body.

2

TRANSPLANTATION

A jiggling began and then continued until she was set down perhaps at the top of her gravesite. Then, although she could not make out any words, whoever had done the digging must be discussing the logistics of where and how to further move her. After a brief rest she was again lifted, not higher than a foot or two, and set upon something else where her box was secured. She knew this as she heard straps being dragged along her box and then a click and another click. Once the straps seemed to be in place it felt as though she was dragged along behind her rescuers, or kidnappers, whoever they might be. It was not a smooth locomotion, but the limited altitude kept her from being anymore fearful than she had been. This much motion in a sightless container would usually have caused her to become nauseous, but she felt nothing in her gut.

However, the journey was difficult. While she may not have been moved very far, it was impossible to say, there was a good deal of bumping, bouncing and dragging. At one point the entire box was moved hastily to the side and dropped a couple of feet before it was

3

straightened up and raised again. Were they trying to avoid detection as they traveled or was this simply a slippery object to manage? Or were they trying to crack the box open? She wondered how many injuries she might sustain before they let her out. Although she could not move on her own, when the box was tilted she would slide into whatever end or side was downhill. Sometimes this movement was rather sudden and painful. Ah, she thought, I am feeling pain; maybe I am not dead.

Eventually they seemed to have arrived at their destination as her box was resting again on a level surface and had not moved for several minutes. It was totally quiet around her. Then she was raised up again and carried bump, bump, and bump, down what must have been a flight of stairs. Here a new scent wafted into her chamber for she no longer smelled the richness of earth but the dank odor of an old cellar. Her box was now resting on a flat surface, and nearby she could hear the sounds of digging but absent was the sound of any voices. Did these people never speak to each other she wondered and when were they going to let her out of this box?

She dozed off and on in her box sometimes experiencing flashes of memories from her past lives. These would come and go. The scent of the cellar brought much of her trauma back to her. She had died in a cellar, maybe this cellar. She had been told by Emily and Will, who are alive part-time in sequence with the katydids and the Goliath Bird Eating Spiders: that the only way to save herself from permanent death at her father's hands was to let the spiders bite her. This would permit her to live and sleep as they did, and all three would remain friends throughout the sequence. So, she did permit the spiders to take her life and then her mind floated as she lived through the grief of seeing her family mourn and bury her.

The most difficult part of the process to watch was seeing that her adoptive parents were so conflicted by her loss. She sensed that they really had loved her but had also been afraid for her and afraid of her. They thought her totally capable of intentionally causing harm to her baby brother, to a classmate and to any critter that got in her way. Yet when they tucked her in at night or braided her hair or helped her with her homework they saw a pretty ten year old girl who had spent much of her life alone. They experienced sadness that she had not felt securely loved and protected but rather discarded in her previous life.

In the late 1800s Grace had been born to a farm family who lived in East Apple, Connecticut. Through no actions of her own, her life and mind were damaged by a strange event of breeding. She was actually conceived by a wonderful woman named Victoria, who had unfortunately been widowed by the man Grace would one day realize was her biological father. Confusing to describe but put simply, although Victoria had a second husband, her first and late husband, had returned through a portal in time, to claim at least a few minutes of sexual pleasure with his wife. Grace's parents were Victoria and this man who had died in the Civil War, a captain named Benjamin Mills. Yet Grace's conception occurred long after Benjamin Mills had passed into "the beyond". When Grace did not, or could not, behave as other children, the problem was thought to lie with her breeding.

By then Victoria was married to Ben's younger brother, Teddy, who was the father of Victoria's first two children. When Teddy realized the nature of Grace's conception he was neither angry nor hurt, given he had courted his brother's widow, but he did understand that something inside a child born to a living woman and a dead man might be off kilter - less than human – perhaps torn between light and dark. And, that was precisely how Grace had behaved: she was very much a child at heart but anything that disturbed or frustrated her ended up with a reaction from Grace far out of proportion to the situation. Being born of a dead father she thought nothing of causing the death of other creatures, or even apparently, her own siblings or friends if given the opportunity.

She had been responsible for the death of puppies belonging to her brother and sister during her time as the child of Victoria and Teddy. She also had planned to cause her siblings grievous harm at that time, and may have turned her back on her grandfather when he needed help. This resulted in the loss of grandfather's life. Thus her biological father, Captain Ben, had reached through the portal and removed Grace from her first life. She was placed in a sort of half life where she was supervised and raised in an orphanage far away from her Connecticut home. And in this half-life she never aged or grew but existed, simply existed. The hope was that her behavior might evolve to a higher sense of "the other," but she still appeared not to see the worth and value of anyone who could be a rival for love or attention. She treated other people as though they were there for her comfort and needs and if they should interfere with her life they had better beware.

But many decades went by and her biological father, functioning through a portal, regretted that Grace had not been able to live her life. He also still loved her mother, Victoria, although Victoria was long dead due to old age and was simply a memory he held dear. The captain had an opportunity to perform a favor for a family in 2020, and in return he asked that they accept Grace as their child; to raise her and to love her. He even warned this family of Grace's troubled past but they were so anxious for the favor that they accepted the condition of doing this favor for the captain. All this was made possible as the family had purchased the captain's portrait painted just before he was lost in the Civil War. They thought it was their good fortune to make contact with another dimension; and to some extent they were correct.

But raising a troubled girl from the late 1800s when she returned to the same area approximately 130 years later was a complicated task. The family invested energy in acclimating Grace to the current times: clothing, language, manners, schooling, history, and especially technology were vastly different. But the most challenging aspect was getting Grace to accept that her former home no longer existed although she could recall where it had been from the turns in the road and the stonewalls which had stood for several hundred years. She also had difficulty accepting that all the people she had known in her former life were gone; most had been dead for many decades. If she wished to communicate with her mother, Victoria, she would need to pray by her gravesite and actually her entire family of origin was gone. Yet Grace remained but ten years old.

So a young couple, Elena Maria and Matthew Nelson, agreed to raise Grace along with their newborn son Mattie. They were initially optimistic that with love and gentle encouragement they could help heal Grace's emotional wounds and support her as she became a happy child. They also engaged Elena Maria's parents in this pursuit of happiness for young Grace whom they learned had once been put to death by her first father. It seemed to them that love would help to compensate her for all she had been through. But they were wrong.

Grace could not forget how horrific her life had been. She could not give up a deep-seated need to be better than others and to control any human being or animal by which she felt threatened. She also had no sense of appropriateness, boundaries or limits on her anger which led her to retaliate in harsh ways upon others. She choked a littler neighbor boy until he was rescued in the midst of her attack; otherwise she might have murdered this child. She saw to it that harm and even death occurred to several pets, and she never expressed remorse or concern over her near killing of baby Mattie.

Elena Maria and Matt had to seek help, once again from the portal, to rid their family from the threat of Grace. They had begun to love her, think of her as a daughter and felt joy when she called them 'mom' and 'dad'. But something continued to be seriously wrong. They hired a psychologist to help them as a family and relished her report that Grace was doing very well until they discovered that Grace had formed a friendship with two people they believed to be dead, who had been buried in their cellar and who had raised giant spiders down there.

The spiders had brought Grace back home to spend her years of dormancy with them, and the two dead/dormant friends, Emily and her son Will.

3

UNDERTAKING

Once Grace and her coffin were safely located at the edge of the dirt floor in the Nelson's cellar, it was time for her to have a "come to Jesus" sort of meeting. In this case it meant that someone needed to remind Grace of all that had transpired and that she was NOT going to wake-up like Sleeping Beauty to live happily-ever-after. Grace had enough spider venom in her to kill many creatures, but in her case it was given to convert her blood to spider serum and permit her to sleep a restorative sleep for seventeen years. At that time, Emily and Will who had already been converted, and the spiders themselves, would all awake in good health and ready to carry on their separate, although brief, lifestyles. Grace could again be a child and roam this house in approximately seventeen years.

Grace had been dead less than a week when the Goliath Bird Eating Spiders dragged her coffin down Cemetery Hill Road on pine branch boughs in the dark of night. Now, just a few hours later, Emily and Will, who had awaited her return, were leaning over the pine box speaking to Grace. They reviewed recent events ending with Grace lowering her wrists for the spiders to bite them after agreeing she would rather live in a sometimes dormant state than to perish altogether if her father were to once more wring her neck. She enjoyed the company of Will and Emily, and now they were explaining that they too would be napping with her and the spiders. The three quasi-human beings were placed in the dirt floor: Grace within her coffin and Emily and Will to their previous spots in the earth next to Grace.

After conducting this burial of what the spiders thought of as their kin, the arachnids then ambled off to disappear down cracks in the floor and stones, spaces where beams could hide them near the ceilings, and a few in the earth to serve as sentries for the human-types. All this transpired within hours of Grace being removed from her grave. By late morning when the caretakers of the cemetery started inspecting the grounds to straighten out any abuse by vandals, they found Grace's grave looking disturbed but not dug-up as it had been. The only other trail on the ground was that of the branches that had both smoothed over the ground and covered line marks which might have hinted at large spider activity should anyone have been astute enough to pick out such marks.

The cemetery workers simply attributed the roughness to animals being curious when they happened upon a fresh grave. They did not think anyone had dug up the body of that poor girl the papers had mentioned. They certainly did not think Giant Goliath Bird Eating Spiders had come to reclaim their kin. With a modest sweeping around her site they left Grace's burial spot pretty much as they had found it. Grace would probably never realize she had, for a few hours, slept in the ground within feet of her dear biological mother, Victoria.

While learning of her situation from Emily and Will, Grace thought to protest that she did not wish to remain in the coffin for so many more years. But, she soon realized that the venom dictated her fate and there was nothing she could do about it. Her eyes became heavy and her breath slowed, she succumbed to deep sleep just as all around her had. Grace went deeply into her dormancy.

Upstairs, above the cellar and above the heads of those who were dormant, Elena Maria moved about the house trying to rearrange her home now that her daughter had died and been buried. She felt a frequent tug at her heart each time she had a moment to consider what might have been if Grace had lived and had not been as disturbed a person; if she could have enjoyed a relationship with her daughter. This melancholia was then replaced with anger that made Elena Maria shake when she recalled how close Grace had gotten to laying baby Mattie on the cellar floor for those hideous spiders to feast upon. That moment in time had been so traumatic that Elena Maria would not go back to mourning the loss of Grace for several hours after each time she recalled Mattie's near death.

And thus, as with much bereavement, there was a mixture of emotions that would not cross a certain barrier. Like oil and water not mixing, or soap being removed by vinegar, Elena Marie could get rid of her moments of weeping over the loss of Grace by recalling how close Grace had come to destroying her baby. This worked well for many weeks.

But as time passed some of Elena Maria's trauma faded. Mattie felt safe in her arms and sleeping by their bedside; she no longer thought of him as vulnerable or herself as somehow not worthy of this beautiful babe. The family of three was a real team and a happy group. She and the dog would push Mattie in the stroller up Cemetery Hill Rd. to take in the crisp spring air and to get exercise. She began to go up the hill as far as the cemetery where she would stroll up to Grace's headstone and say a little prayer for her troubled daughter.

She prayed that Grace was sleeping with the angels and promised to teach Mattie that he had a big sister who had died when Mattie was a baby but that they loved her in memory. She hoped none of the neighbors would one day feel compelled to tell Mattie about his evil sister. Elena Marie did not think of her as evil but as damaged and unwell.

Sometimes Elena Maria went into in the basement. She stored a few pantry items and some wine down there because it was a cooler temperature than the upper stories of the house. She didn't like to stay in the cellar for very long as it would remind her of the awful fright with Mattie and with their loss of Grace. She also believed that Will was buried in the dirt. For a time the police had believed that photographs on an old game camera contained pictures of an odd couple living in their cellar and associating with Grace. However, experts that the lawyer who worked for Elena Maria and Matt had hired to defend them from any accusations of causing their daughter harm debunked the notion that these shadowy photos were more than double images; photos taken at another time. One can never tell when these motion sensitive cameras will click an image.

So Elena Maria did not long remain in the basement. But sometimes when she was down there she almost sensed the presence of others, maybe even Grace. Her husband, a psychology professor, told Elena Maria that she was too susceptible to old memories. These memories triggered feelings in her that made her think she was actually receiving messages when in fact no messages existed. The circumstances conjured up memories that confused Elena Maria when she was feeling low. She did not argue with Matt, she figured he was probably correct, but she still did not go into the cellar unless she absolutely had to!

It was a time when the COVID virus had begun to fade somewhat in importance; most everyone had been vaccinated. Just poor baby Mattie was not yet protected, but that might come soon. Also, much of her family in Italy had to be careful due to a resurgence of the virus in alternate forms. This worried everyone especially her mother who still had so many close relatives over there.

It was a time when Matthew and Elena Maria could consider putting their house on the market. It would be easy to show the place now that restrictions were lowered; many people were anxious to have homes in the country after being confined, in some cases, for months in city apartments; and the dramatic stories of the deaths within their home on Cemetery Hill Road would have faded and look less horrible as compared to COVID deaths and fears.. They were getting more serious about this move forward. Although they loved the house and its many beautiful fireplaces, they would still like to shake themselves free of memories like the spiders in the cellar.

Matt was finishing his breakfast about two weeks later and reading aloud some selling tips from their realtor, Adam, when Elena Maria grabbed the side of the sink and then ran for the bathroom. She thought she'd better check with the doctor later on that day, but she was now convinced that she was again pregnant. Very close in age to baby Mattie but a blessing where there had been sorrow; she also thought she had best return to church as she had a lot of prayers to make in gratitude for all they had. And maybe it was not the best time to be packing up such a large house and hunting for a new place with two babies to carry around.

4

SLITHER

That last bump down the cellar stairs had been a bit rougher than the coffin could well handle. It ever so slightly put a crack between the casket's cover and the seal at the lip of the box. Grace had never had the kind of personality to "just go along with what was good for her." Indeed, in death she remained a restless spirit, and the notion of being quiet, dormant, for some seventeen years did not settle well with her already disturbed psyche. Thus for her a solid sleep was impossible. Grace would periodically open her eyes wide and just test the environment for anything that she could sense. Her eyes were all that she could move, but when the brain woke up just enough to trigger her unhappiness, she would force her eyes open to see what she could see.

Three weeks after arriving in the cellar, down the hill, but still on Cemetery Hill Road she popped open her orbs and would have gasped if she could have. Somehow, between the cracks at the lid of the coffin, the fact that two other bodies were also in that area and that simple-minded spiders had performed the burial, she beheld a little light! It was a shallow gravesite at best and thus the dirt surrounding Grace's coffin was sparse enough to be permeated by some meager amount of sun. Grace observed light for the first time since her death.

Then, she fell back into her uneasy slumber; her brain was dreaming of escape, ways to leave the coffin and move among the living as though she belonged with them. She reasoned such a thing might be possible if her father did not catch sight of her, for surely he would again see to it that she could not live. Towards the goal of becoming part of the world she thought to build her muscle strength. Whenever her brain triggered a bit of arousal she would not only open her eyes but she would try to clench her fists. Unfortunately, the venom with which she had been infused would not permit her any freedom of movement save the eyelids.

More time went by; perhaps it was summer in the outside world. Once she thought she heard her mother Elena Maria walk by this gravesite but she said not a word of greeting or of prayer. Of course she would think Grace was still buried up at the top of Cemetery Hill; "Ha, little does she know" thought Grace. Then her heavily drugged blood forced her back to sleep.

It happened to rain very hard that night, so hard that the old stone foundation of the cellar leaked several streams of water. This happened often enough that the cellar had a sump pump which automatically began to pump water out a drain so that the basement would not get too badly flooded. It was churning away pumping out water much of the night. Also with this volume of water little creatures which slept in the cellar would become disturbed. Salamanders, reds, earwigs, small spiders and even mice had to flee for their lives. And on this particular night a copperhead snake floated for a moment and then dove into the dirt seeking shelter.

The copperhead moved between some bones and boards within the dirt until it came upon a gap between boards leading into a cool, dry, and dark place. It slithered over to Grace and decided to dry off there and wait for bugs to come by. It was in no hurry; then Grace, sensing a change in her atmosphere, popped her eyes open again. There was a blur beginning at her left eye and running down her nose and over her lips where it disappeared somewhere under her chin. The parts that were too close to her eye remained a blur but just before it disappeared she realized that she was focusing in on a snake! Grace did not like snakes and especially being invaded by them like this. She tried with all her might to scream but nothing would arise from her body, no sound at all. But there was the tiniest movement with simultaneous muscle tightening in her arms.

The snake did not like people nor did it like surprises, and especially it did not care for the sense that something had been waiting to surprise it. So as it slithered off of Grace's body it snapped its head around and gave Grace a wide-open, jaw dropping, fang puncturing bite near her carotid artery. She felt this bite and its impact on her entire being. Her toes curled and her hands formed fists and she emitted a sound that was something like "Errrrr!" Then she again fell into a dead sleep.

The biggest surprise was that there had been an experiment years back looking at the effects of Giant Goliath Bird Eating Spider's venom and that of rattlesnakes and copperheads. The antidote for spider venom carried by researchers into the jungles was made from snake venom. Either could kill an individual but taken together they tended to neutralize the effects of the other. Grace had just accidentally been given serum that might allow her to wake up and enjoy a normal life, at least for Grace. But at this moment she lay there not knowing what had hit her. She slept without stirring, or blinking, or even having a thought pass through her usually overactive brain. She slept as though dead.

And six days later she woke up and thought "How strange, I think I need to pee!" Now dead people don't urinate, and those in dormant states do not urinate either. Maybe a hibernating animal might occasionally have such needs but even this is rare. Grace was suddenly, acutely aware that her kidneys were functioning. "Oh, great she thought. Now what the heck do I do?"

She tried to move and for the first time in months her body responded. She could shift her weight from side to side by hunching her shoulders. She could contract, although very weakly, her muscles and she could feel the end of the coffin with her feet. "Holy shit" she quietly uttered for her vocabulary had always been inappropriate for a young girl, "I'm alive and I'm speaking!"

Grace lay back down to rest and to collect her thoughts. She would need a strategy: first, to get out of this coffin; and second, to figure out how to live in this house without her parents knowing she was here and alive. And, especially, her biological father in the portal must not sense her presence, for he could find her and dispatch her from anywhere. She did not like this dying business, and should she now survive yet another demise she was in no hurry to return to the dead.

She reasoned that the coffin must be weakest in the place where she saw the light and where apparently the snake slithered in to see her. So perhaps she could attack that area, but, and this was a big but, the weight of the earth on top of the coffin lid would be impossible for her to budge in her weakened state. Still, she had seen a bit of light emanating from that area so maybe if she had a wedge and gave a push with all her might, maybe just maybe, she could get free.

She felt the top of the coffin through what remained of her shroud. No loose boards to use as a wedge. Then she managed to wriggle a shoe off her foot and through some tears in the cloth of the shroud. Then she would have to find the strength to get to the foot of the coffin and hunch herself up placing the shoe as a wedge in the crack between the lid and the top of the coffin. It would take so much strength that Grace had to assume she would have but one try before her energy ran out. She rested.

After forcing her mind to be alert and getting her heart to pick up its tempo through sheer concentration, she made a sound something like a muscle man about to chop his hands through thick stacks of wood, and then she dove to the foot of her casket, wrenching the shoe into the crack and pushing upward using her back and all her adrenalin. The wood groaned then felt a bit rubbery and then cracked. Grace had heaved herself up, through and out of the coffin. She spilled out and onto the cellar floor in a heap of loose soil wetting her pants and laughing with joy as she landed on the concrete.

5

THE FAMILY GROWS

Elena Maria was elated when later that same day the doctor called to confirm that she was indeed pregnant. He asked if she thought she'd be able to handle two infants at one time. She was proud to tell him yes, she thought that she could, and if necessary they could afford a nanny. "After all," she added, "some women have twins or more, and they find a way to manage although I am certain it is not easy."

As soon as the doctor rang off she called Matt to confirm the good news. They committed to celebrating that evening by ordering a restaurant meal and Matt would pick it up on his way home. COVID had taught them caution regarding restaurant dining which they would continue to follow especially with another baby expected. Then Elena Maria called her parents and was delighted when her mother answered the phone. It felt right that her mom would be the second person to learn this great news. But, not counting the doctor and of course, Elena Maria, her mom was the third person to learn about the pregnancy.

It happened that Grace, having just "fallen back into the world of the living" had made her way upstairs in Matt and Elena Maria's bedroom when she heard the telephone ring. Curious as to what was going on with the family she gently picked up the receiver, covered her mouth and just listened. It was in this manner that she learned of another impending sibling.

This had happened after Grace rested on the cellar floor for several minutes. While experiencing near hysterics, she realized that she must start to function again as a living being. This would include getting some dry clothing and eating, for she had been without food for a very long time, although while dormant, not much energy was required. Fortunately, her memory was intact, and she knew that there was a trapdoor from the cellar up into the bedroom closet attached to her parents' bedroom.

She rose from the concrete on unsteady feet but made her way over to the long string which pulled the staircase down to the basement. She shakily managed this task and then slowly ascended the stairs until she was in that closet. Here she had a sensation of finding a treasure trove for most of her needs were right at hand. Her mother's (Elena Maria's) three quarter length pants would serve Grace well as slacks; Grace did not mind having loose fitting tops so she helped herself to several sweaters and a pair of Elena Maria's sneakers which were only a bit too big.

Next she must proceed with great caution for the underwear and socks she required would be in the bedroom itself set inside a dresser drawer. This meant Grace had to slowly open the bedroom closet door, listen carefully and then tiptoe into the bedroom. She was able to manage all this and when she stood near the bureau, she could hear Elena Maria's voice coming up the staircase as she spoke on the phone with her own mother. Knowing that they stayed on the phone for extended periods of time, Grace ventured into the adjoining bathroom long enough to have a good wash. She then placed the facecloth into a bag and planned to take it back into the cellar. She would use it again and this removed a piece of evidence that might be too noticeable to be ignored.

Finally Grace returned to the bedroom, scooped up the socks and underpants she felt would not be missed, and scurried back through the closet, down the trapdoor ladder and once again into the basement. After arriving in this "safe place" Grace made her way to the base of the chimney which formed a little room hidden from the cellar by four stone walls. There was a small opening in one wall and she bent down and entered this area. Here she would store her clothing and any supplies she might need. Also in this chamber were the books and games Emily used to play with and to entertain Will. They were still there and only a little dusty. Perhaps Grace could entertain herself with some of this material although it felt lonely to even look at these things without her two companions. She would think about these matters later, there was much else to be resolved, and number one was hunger.

It was Grace's lucky day: not only had she arisen from the dead and found her way out of the tomb, but she had garnered the clothing she needed, washed and found a somewhat secure hiding place for her things. And, it even crossed her mind, that she should be excited at the prospect of having a new baby brother or sister. Topping this all off, as she looked out the small basement window, she could see her neighbor, complete with three children, loading up in the car and heading out their driveway. This should mean that their house was empty for at least the next hour.

Grace didn't waste any time. She crouched down like an animal on all fours and scurried through the long grass surrounding the path to the neighbors' side door. As was their habit, the door wasn't even locked. Grace moved hastily to the kitchen. She was so ravenous that she stood inside the refrigerator door and ate from whatever she fancied using her fingers. In this manner she devoured cold chicken, cold but cooked green beans, mashed potatoes, and brownies – heavenly brownies. She was careful to move things around on their plates or dishes so that no one would readily notice the missing food. When it came to the brownies she ate one and placed two in her pocket for later. She found a knife and cut the remaining brownies into smaller pieces that would almost occupy the plate as much as had the original batch.

They had plenty of milk so she snatched an opened container following this up by taking a plastic bowl, a soup spoon, and a box of cereal that was way back inside the cupboard. She then looked around to determine if there was anything else which she needed or anything she ought to clean up. Feeling she was in the clear she scooted back out the side door narrowly missing the family as they drove in on the other side of the house.

Grace was so full that she felt she might pop open, but she was also pleased with herself as she entered her chimney home. She was alive, clothed and now had food enough to get through the next morning. Still, she began to wonder, how long will I manage like this? Then she recalled how she had fed the spiders for weeks by stealing food from her parents' refrigerator. Why couldn't she sneak upstairs every night and just take food. Of course she had eventually been caught at this but if she continued to only feed herself the volume of missing food would not be too large. Elena Maria made so much food that they would probably never miss it. And so, Grace began to relax thinking that she had plenty of time to figure out how she could take care of herself or where she might go.

There was one thing she hadn't thought of, however. One thing that she could not get around at least not for very long; and because of the trouble it would cause, this was one thing she could not deal with in a harsh way. His name was Scruffy and he was the family dog. He knew Grace and he knew her scent; as soon as she returned to life, especially doing something as strong as urinating on the floor, Scruffy had known she was around.

It was Grace's good fortune that Scruffy had been with Elena Maria much of the day. They had gone together with the baby to see the doctor first thing in the morning, followed by fish sticks for lunch which had a strong odor of their own thus at least temporarily overpowering the smell Grace had made. But since lunch had been cleaned up and aired out, Grace had entered the upstairs of the house before she was bathed; and had reentered the house with food, Scruffy was becoming increasingly restless.

Grace heard the dog whining at the top of the kitchen stairs and scratching at the door that would lead down to her. It suddenly dawned on the child that this would be trouble. She looked around and saw the dirt was askew where she had crashed through her coffin. She found an old piece of cardboard and used it to shovel and pat down the earth that had been disturbed. She mixed the dirt which she had made wet, though it now was dry, in with the other soil to help mask any odor and also pushed the cardboard deeply into the soil. Then she went back to hide in her chimney room and see what, if anything, would happen next.

6

DIGGING SPIDERS

Scruffy did not cease his barking and scratching simply because Grace had tidied up the cellar dirt a bit. Finally, Matt returned home and immediately asked Elena Maria what all the ruckus was about with the dog. She had been too busy passing on her good news over the phone with the baby in her arms to even notice the dog.

Matt's response was to open the cellar door off the kitchen and follow the dog downstairs with a flashlight. He called back to her "I'll take him down to check things out just in case we have a rodent running around, and I should check the sump pump anyway after all that rain." And then he descended those old cellar stairs.

Scruffy went immediately to the dirt pile that they knew had once contained skeletons but that now they believed to only hold the very old and dry body of Emily. Hardly a bone worth picking old boy Matt thought. But something in that spot had stirred the dog up, and he was even more excited as he stood upon it. The barking and snapping gave way to digging until Matt yelled "No boy, down,

24

bad dog." Then patting Scruffy's head he said "We can't have you digging things up all over the floor. Just come away from there."

Tail between his legs, for he rarely was told that he was a 'bad dog'; Scruffy followed his master to the sump pump for an inspection by flashlight. While Matt was concentrating on some thicker materials that might clog up the drain during future floods, Scruffy hurried back to the dirt floor and commenced an all out battle with the dirt. By the time Matt got over to the dog to call him off and probably repeat the reprimand, Scruffy had uncovered the rather droopy body of a Giant Bird Eating Arachnid. This, of course, was the sentinel spider which had buried Grace and then imbedded itself into the soil. It had been intended to guard her body, but it was not exempt from dormancy, and had soon gone into a stupor not even knowing its charge had arisen from her resting place.

"Ah," said Matt, "Not a bad dog. How on earth did you smell this monster still in the house? Well, I'll go out to the barn and get a shovel. Come on boy." And they left. A few minutes later Matt returned alone with the tool thinking that Scruffy might interfere. He carried the limp spider outside where he wacked the creature a couple of times and then flung the now lifeless body into the trash. Feeling very manly he went into the house to tell Elena Maria how he had protected their home with, of course, the help of Scruffy.

For the moment Grace was safe and the dog was mollified, but she would have to find a way to cover her tracks: not only the sight of herself, or signs of what she had taken, but her olfactory signals as well. This time she had hidden in the corner of the room at the base of chimney by covering herself in old hay. The hay had been there for years. It had been added to help collect moisture from a small chimney leak before the owners of that time could afford to repair the mortar. Old damp straw had enough odor of its own, and the soil had captivated the dog long enough, that Grace could mask herself, this time.

But deep inside the mind of a dog something else was happening. He might be content for the moment, and his family was happy with him, but he did not feel settled. The reason for this was that he recognized the smell of urine from a mile away. After all, eighty percent of a dog's brain is his nose. And in this case he knew it was human pee, not something a stupid spider had excreted. And in this case he further knew who had produced the wetness, it was Grace, the girl who had lived here for awhile and then gone away. Well, he had news for everyone, she was back. Grace was living in this house again, so he and Sybil, the cat she had nearly starved to death by shutting her up in a barn cupboard, had better be on the alert – this could be trouble.

Scruffy went to find the cat to commiserate; they would need to have each other's backs. He found her in the kitchen licking a tiny bit of cream and was given a large Milk Bone. It seemed that the family had something to celebrate so it was just as well they did not yet know about Grace or that would spoil their fun.

Soon enough it was bedtime and the family settled in for the night. When the household had been watching out for a strange man who kept coming in while no one was home, about seven years back in Scruffy's mind, they had allowed Scruffy to sleep wherever he wanted to serve as sort of a guard dog. But since this man had drugged Scruffy causing him to fail at his mission, they had gone back to the old crate-trained method and he was again closed in for the night although Sybil would often crawl in with him. He had never imagined that cats could be so nice.

As he settled in for the night he heard Elena Maria ask Matt where their big quilt had gone to, to which he replied "I have no idea."

"Odd," she said, "I had just picked it up from the dry cleaner and it was still wrapped in plastic. The plastic is here but no quilt."

Matt replied, "Did your first pregnancy make you forgetful too?"

Scruffy couldn't hear his mistress's response but they were then both laughing. It must be that the baby was nursing, not sleeping, or they would have been more quiet thought the dog before he fell asleep.

It was probably an hour after all lights were out that Grace made her move. First she crept up from the cellar steering widely around the dog's crate and tiptoeing very gently. She was carrying a pail and took it into the bathroom and flushed. She was then in there a few minutes before she came out washing her hands and making a bee-line for the refrigerator. She knew where the plastic bags were kept, filled one with a little of everything, took a bottle of ginger ale, followed by some paper towels, and then descended again into the cellar. At the last minute she remembered to grab the pail and seemed greatly relieved that she had done so. Thus Grace passed her first full day of life in this her third try at attempting to survive among others. She was hoping that one of these times she would actually acquire an age beyond that of ten. And this time she not only steered clear of the dog but of her father whose face hung in a portrait in the parlor, at least for now.

The dog slept through Grace's relatively quiet and well timed adventure onto the first floor, but when he arose the next morning he began sniffing the floor from the cellar door to the bathroom and then to the refrigerator and all around the kitchen. He knew Grace had been there and he was just sorry he had missed her, but he became determined not to let this happen to him again, he would endeavor to remain awake the next night.

Grace had caused him and Sybil a great deal of concern and he knew she had frightened his people. He thought she might be the one exception to the rule that you don't bite people; in fact he was sure of it.

7

CRUMBS IN THE ATTIC

Grace used the quilt, and a pillow she had taken from the guest bedroom to make a temporary bed on top of the hay in the chimney area. She found this fairly comfortable, and it provided a sense of security from that troublesome dog. Although she had slept long hours while dormant, this slumber provided a different kind of healing rest, one that cleaned out her human blood from the day's workout for survival. She slept like; you should forgive the term, the dead. But when she woke up she again feared the dog even though she had found a way to cover up the scent of what she put in the bucket.

After eating her cereal and the last of the milk, she began planning for her safety. She thought of spending more time in the attic but knew that getting there would be difficult. The trapdoor would be impossible to access at night as it was entered through her parents' bedroom; still she feared the dog more than she feared them and she wasn't sure how well old Scruffy was sleeping these days. He was still a beautiful liver colored Springer Spaniel but perhaps not as quick

CYNTHIA HERBERT-BRUSCHI ADAMS

as he had once been. Anyway, if she wanted to use that large attic space which contained two full windows, providing her with quite a lookout post, she would have to get from the cellar to the second floor to enter the attic through the guest room closet. So many hazards she thought!

But maybe she could set the attic up in a way that would allow her to treat it as her primary area. The cellar had been so easy to slip in and out of, even crossing over to the neighbors' yard yesterday, yet she had nearly been caught so how good could that really be? Today's expedition would be to the attic just to consider it as a possibility. Certainly no one would be sending the dog into the attic to get him out of the way of unexpected company, although there was little company during the pandemic. And Matt would not be going up to the attic to check on pipes, or pumps or to bring up canned vegetables. Still, Grace was reluctant to go as the attic made it much more difficult for her to listen in on what people were talking about and when she was in her parents' bedroom she could actually listen in on the landline.

She waited patiently most of the morning then finally saw Elena Maria pull the baby carriage out of the side door. Of course Mattie was inside the carriage, big Matt was at the University, and Scruffy had his leash attached to the stroller's handle. She could get up to the attic and see what was what. Her first move was into the kitchen where she grabbed a couple bites of cheese and took two slices of bread, stopped in the bathroom, and then hurried to the guestroom and up the attic stairs. It was so peaceful in the attic that she enjoyed a relaxing breath of air for the first time in a long time.

She had forgotten about the cedar closet up here which made a whole entire room as it offered closet space on three walls with a door to help keep the dust out. It had the strong odor of its cedar wood paneling but she found this pleasant and a safety against Scruffy's keen sense of smell.

While this was a pleasant find, the biggest surprise was the contents of the closet. It held numerous folded blankets and quilts, an assortment of wool clothing which Elena Maria must just have put away, and winter outerwear such as boots, gloves, scarves, hats and coats. It did not take the ten-year-old long to fashion up a grand bed on the closet floor. She padded the bed with coats then layered the quilts upon them and then placed a winter bathrobe where she could swing it over herself for a blanket. She stuffed several hats inside one another and beheld a perfect pillow.

The last thing she discovered was little less than a miracle. It was a commode probably used by some elderly guest in case they could not make it to the bathroom. While it would not provide a source of water for Grace, she could use it and then empty and clean it whenever the coast was clear. She thought if there was a refrigerator she would never have to leave!

But, of course, by evening she was desperately hungry and thirsty and could barely wait for the family to quiet down so that she could find food and water. She began her ascent from the attic to the second floor and then made her way stealthily down a hall so that she could go down the stairs to the kitchen without passing by her parent's bedroom.

Everything seemed to work out well until she opened the first floor kitchen door and heard a very low pitched growl coming from Scruffy's crate. She stepped into the kitchen quickly but carefully pulled the door closed behind her. Then in the sweetest voice she could muster she said "Hi Scruffy boy, is that you? I have missed you so much. Let me unlock your cage so we can play." And she made her way to the crate still speaking as though she was his long lost and adoring mistress.

But all Scruffy heard were sounds giving him distress. He knew this person and what she was capable of doing. When she got to the lip of the crate he lunged making the container move forward as he snapped at her through the metal grates. Then he continued to snap and growl rather fiercely setting off a commotion and involving Sybil in the hissing at this intruder. Grace was wondering which way she should turn when she heard her father's footsteps on the stairs coming right toward them. With no time to spare she was flying down the cellar stairs to ensconce herself within the chimney room. Grace was shaking like an electric mixer on high speed by the time she crawled into that familiar corner then covered herself with hay.

Scruffy was right on the door behind her but Grace had shut it too quickly for him to reach her. He lost time while Matt was releasing him from the crate as Matt came to see what was wrong with the dog. So once again Matt took the flashlight, and once again they looked in the cellar in vain. When they returned to the first floor Grace looked like a frightened ten-year-old girl. She was huddled in the corner covered with straw and bawling her eyes out. Suddenly this adventure seemed far from fun, it seemed grim.

Matt sat patiently upstairs with his dog. In fact the dog was in his lap whining. Scruffy wanted so badly to talk and explain what was going on. Scruffy loved Matt and wished to prove his loyalty by earning it. Matt said, "I believe there is something real that is bothering you, old pal, and tonight may not be our night, but I will help you to find whatever it is that has upset you so. I'll leave you loose the rest of the night, and we'll go on a hunt sometime Saturday and turn this place upside down until we find that squirrel or whatever has got you. Now let's get some rest and try not to wake up the baby."

And so Matt went upstairs to retire again and Scruffy circled a rug six times and lay down with a 'humph'. While they were resting Grace was continuing to feel dehydrated. In desperation she crept out of the house in the dark when there were also no lights on at the neighbors, and crawled through their house on all fours. When she got to the kitchen she literally crept up the side of the refrigerator opening it slowly to avoid noise and then drinking lemonade directly from the pitcher.

The liquid helped her regain her senses, and she stopped and cleaned up any of it that had spilled or dripped. She even wiped inside the refrigerator and then found a small bottle that she could take with her. Next she selected cheese, cold cuts, and a cooked chicken leg. Finally she went to the crisper and took two apples and some carrots. She managed to get enough of this into her pockets so that she could have one arm free to guide herself back out into the dark night.

As she made her way across the driveway headed for her basement home, for she certainly wouldn't dare try to return to the attic tonight, a pair of eyes from the neighbors' house peered out the side window following her progress. Had she been more observant and less pressured she would have detected that she was being observed. How curious that someone would behold the sight of this starving child and say nothing, just let her go, but that is what happened this time.

8

GOTCHA

Once she curled up in her chimney corner amidst the hay Grace fell into an exhausted sleep. While she slept she dreamt of being chased by three dogs until these dogs had her cornered in a tree. One was clearly a pit bull and must have been bred to fight, another was brindle colored with a heavy chest and approximately the size and weight of the pit bull, the third looked more like it had returned to its ancestor the wolf. It was tall and had a rough coat around the head making it lion-like. Its mouth was the largest with a snarling grin right out of the wild. Little Red Riding Hood would have been paralyzed with fear.

The dogs then surrounded the base of the tree and continued snapping and barking. Finally, one of the dogs was so over-wrought that it literally leapt into the branch nearest to Grace and was snapping at her face. She clung to the tree shivering and crying. "Go away! Please go away!" she sobbed.

Then Grace woke up. Light shone into the basement from one of the small windows as she could see a beam of sunshine reflected up from the concrete floor outside the chimney room opening. She had slept through until morning. Although the dream toward the end of her sleep was very scary, she was amazed at the time which had passed without her being up and restless. She wiped tears from her face, urinated into her pail and covered the top with a chemical housecleaning product and then a lid, and washed her face and hands with cold water from a jug of water she had secured the previous day.

Nothing was perfect, but it could be worse she told herself, and then ate the stale bread and mushy cheese she had commandeered from last night's raid at the neighbor's house. She drank a little of her precious water and began planning her day. First she would have to determine where all members of the household were at this moment, especially that damnable dog. Grace was a ten-year-old in some ways, but her vocabulary was peppered with cuss words spanning two centuries and offending any adult within earshot. She had actually just gone easy on Scruffy.

As Grace peered out the basement window which ran along the driveway she saw Matt's car pull out of the yard. So it's probably around eight she thought, if he is now heading to the University. She then walked around the cellar a few times thinking this exercise might help prepare her for the day. Finally, she caught a glimpse of a blur passing by the window and rushed to happily confirm that Elena Maria had again taken the dog for a walk along with the baby. Grace smiled; maybe this would be a good day.

She walked up the cellar staircase and gingerly opened the door into the kitchen, carefully, just-in-case. She said "Hello" and delighted when there was no answer. Then she rushed to the bathroom doing all she needed to do and washing very thoroughly, even getting her hair with a little soap, under the faucet. Next, she put water into a large empty bottle from the recycling bin, grabbed more paper towels, and ate all she could stuff into her mouth from the refrigerator. She was careful not to finish off any one dish and always moved the food around so that it might appear to require all the space available.

Finally, she searched for cookies in the cupboards, came up with a partial package and decided she could take it as whoever looked would assume the other guy had finished it. Then she checked everything; took her rinsed out pail for the cellar, her new water jug, and headed down the cellar stairs to safety.

Once there she tried to decide what to do with her time. At least Emily and Will had each other when they were out of dormancy but she had no one without them. Of course, she also had to consider that this was not dormancy; this was a "forever" life so maybe she should not settle for hanging out in the 'crawl spaces' of other people's lives – maybe she had to decide what moves to make and how she might plan a future. These were overwhelming thoughts since Grace really only had a child's mentality but now she had a very grown-up concern without parents to guide her.

Grace decided to wait until after lunch to think of what she could do today. Matt sometimes came home for lunch, especially since little Mattie had been born, and if they were sitting in the kitchen she would be able to listen in on the conversation. Grace figured their talk would probably inform her of when and where they each would be for at least the rest of the day.

When Matt arrived home Grace was perched near the top of the cellar stairs ready to listen in on the family's schedule. She moved a little closer to the door as she heard Matt say that Scruffy had wanted to explore the barn so he was staying out for a while. Matt said he was glad the dog would get some exercise out there as he had been acting oddly the last few days and Matt hoped the air would do him good.

Before too much else could be discussed Elena Maria opened the refrigerator door to prepare their lunch while Matt was giving the baby a bottle. She exclaimed "I must be reliving our old trauma; you know, when Emily, Will and Grace were stealing food to feed those horrible arachnids? I swear half of what we had leftover from last night's supper is gone and you were at work all morning."

"Are you certain?" said Matt, "We didn't have a big bedtime snack, did we?"

"No, Matt, we made a bowl of popcorn, remember, to eat with Netflix, and then I tossed the last few kernels out into the yard for the birds as we were going to bed. Since Scruffy was in the house it seemed our feathered friends might have a chance before he did."

"I do remember that," said Matt. "It makes me uneasy to hear this just as it worries you. Well, let's pay attention for a few days and see what happens."

On the staircase Grace's face caved in; she looked as sad as a kid when their trip to Disney has been cancelled or their mother says "no dessert for a month." Actually, Grace had just heard, no more food for you, within that statement of them needing to 'pay attention'.

As soon as she could, Grace got off the stairs, and hid in the chimney room. After almost never shedding tears in her lives, Grace was now crying for the second consecutive day. This being human was turning out to be pretty difficult. She sulked in her bedding most of the rest of the day. The only recourse she could think of was that the neighbors never locked their door. She figured she had no choice but to sneak over there again tonight. Well, at least, she thought, I am already in the cellar.

When Grace's family went to bed and the dog was at last upstairs for the night, Grace began looking across the driveway at the neighbor's home. Very soon after her house was quiet, Grace noticed that all the lights were out over there too. She grabbed a little paper and snuck out into the bushes on the edge of her folks' property that abutted the neighbors'. She went into those bushes far enough to be off the path, and she relieved herself leaving the paper under a few leaves. Then she crept onto the neighbor's side entry and again gave thanks that the door was unlocked.

Once in the house she went to the kitchen sink and washed her face and hands. This would have to be it for her nighttime bath which she used to love. Then she went to open the refrigerator and would have screamed when a large hairy arm pushed the door shut before she could get it open, but the other hand of this person was clamped over her mouth: It wasn't gentle and it pulled her close to its body. She could hardly breathe as it lifted her up and whispered in her ear.

"I've been watching you, girly, and I know you are a thief. I don't know what else you are, but I do know you look an awful lot like that crazy girl from next door who died not too long ago. So, whoever you are, and whatever your game is doesn't matter to me, but I want to have a little fun with you, and you had better keep your mouth shut. I will let you go but we are going to play a little bit, then I will feed you and you can leave. Just be quiet. Do you understand?"

Grace was terrified. She thought she knew what that fun might involve and she wanted nothing to do with it, but she nodded her head 'all right' so he would let her go. However, as soon as his hands were free, the father of her former friends, the little neighbor children, forced his mouth on hers pushing his tongue into her mouth and groping her private parts with his hands. He was rough and she was horrified. She started thinking maybe God was punishing her for the many wicked things she had done to others, and she must deserve this.

Grace couldn't help but squirm under his weight and due to his roughness. This appeared to make him even happier until he gave a great guttural sigh and let her go. He pulled away from her saying "Help yourself and then get out, but I want you back here tomorrow night or there will be trouble."

Grace reached into the refrigerator and took a whole container of cooked hamburger casserole and then ran for the door.

9

THE DISGUISE

It was hours before Grace could fall asleep. She was so shaken by the neighbor's savage behavior toward her that she was at first in shock and then so angry that she fantasized killing him in several gruesome ways. However, a rational side emerged which told her that if she killed this man the investigation was certain to involve neighbors and that she would be discovered, if not as the murderer then at least as a living corpse. She then turned her mental energy into trying to find a way to eat that did not involve going next door.

Grace's plan emerged as one in which she would have to acquire money, a disguise, and actually walk into the little market about a half mile away. She reasoned that not that many people in town really knew her, those that did knew that she was dead, and if she dressed well enough who would dare cry out, "Aren't you that child who let herself be poisoned by spiders?"

And so, the next morning she patiently waited for the house to empty. Finally, Matt went to work taking Scruffy with him. Perhaps Scruffy was going to the veterinarian; in any case he was gone. Then

Elena Maria and the baby went out with the stroller. As soon as they rounded the corner of the driveway Grace ran to the cord for the trapdoor and pulled it down, then ran up to her parents' bedroom.

She hunted for a fresh pair of short pants that might look a bit more grownup than the denim pair she had been wearing. She finally decided on a beige pair, and then found a modest pullover and a matching sweater. Now she explored the scarves Elena Maria kept in her top drawer. There was a simple pale floral one that would have to work. Finally, she went into the bathroom and looked in the backs of drawers for makeup Elena Maria was probably not using very often and was, therefore, unlikely to miss.

She grabbed her cache of finds and was heading for the trapdoor when she heard a noise downstairs. Elena Maria was cooing, "You poor little baby, such a wet diaper, you must have been holding it for a long time. Well, mommy will get you all cleaned off and then we can have our nice walk."

So, the kid had sprung a leak, Grace thought to herself, well, I'll be out of the way in two seconds. As she started down the steps which were attached to the trap door, they made a loud crack and groan. Grace stood absolutely still and did not even breathe. When she heard no sound from Elena Maria and no rush of feet coming towards her, she continued to the safety of the basement. Once she was on the cellar floor Grace very gently sent the trapdoor back up to its resting place two floors above.

It was then that she remembered that she had no money. "Rats," she said out loud, "I meant to raid their change jug and Elena Maria's wallet if her purse is up there. When she goes out I guess I'll go up again." And she scowled, for she was getting hungry and very anxious about the shopping and the disguise she would have to now assemble.

It was midmorning before Grace had gathered many quarters and a ten dollar bill from her parents' bedroom. She was desperately hungry and anxious to see how far her money would go. It was a cool enough day that the scarf would not look out of place, Grace reckoned, but she certainly hoped nothing would pull it off her head as she feared she might be recognizable if her hair was to be exposed. She had applied a little foundation to cover some of her freckles and just a hint of lip-stick again in an attempt to be less childlike. She was ready to go, adding a mask as COVID dictated, she was as secure as she could be. In fact, Grace wondered why she had worried so much about the makeup as the mask hid most of her face especially with the scarf on.

She checked as best she could to be certain that the coast was clear, and then she went around the barn and down a different path to the road so that it would not be obvious to any passerby from where Grace had emerged. Then she moved her legs as fast as she dared, not wishing to look like she was running, until she was at the little store. She was in luck, only one other customer.

Grace entered and decided to examine everything before making her decisions. Whatever she chose had to be edible without cooking, sustainable without refrigeration, and tasty. Finally Grace decided on bread, peanut butter, raisins, and two chocolate bars. She had added it all up in her head and believed that even with a slight tax on the candy, she had enough money. She just wanted to pay for it all and get out of the store before someone came in who knew her. Unfortunately, the guy at the register wanted to kid around with her a bit and even ask questions. She knew she might well be coming back here so she endeavored to be polite but unremarkable; there was no sense in standing out in anyone's mind.

After what Grace considered to be just a little pitiful banter, she was released to the world with a bag full of food and a quarter left over. She practically skipped towards home until she remembered that she wanted to simply blend in and not seem too happy or sad for this town. She pulled out a slice of bread and stopped briefly to eat that for energy before she continued a now slower sojourn home. All she could think was that the 'fat fuck' of a father next door would be mighty surprised when she did not show up tonight. She hoped he'd be peering out the door searching for her all night long. And she was certain he would not make trouble for her as he would obviously cause himself a great deal of trouble if he did so.

Grace was feeling pretty smart until she saw a woman in the distance pushing a baby stroller and headed right for her! She saw a path that led to the church parking lot and took it. For the next half hour she hid next to the Congregationalist's trash cans and tried to enjoy her bread dipped into the peanut butter. Then she slowing looked back around to where she had been going before she saw her mother coming. Again, no one was out there although she would now be returning to an occupied house. Well, thought Grace, I won't try this too often.

When she reached her destination she walked past the house and then circled back through a wooded path ending up behind their barn. She inched around the edge of the barn until she could see the house. Just when she thought that it was safe to run to the cellar door, Scruffy came charging at her. He must have returned from the veterinarian's while she was communing with the trash cans. Grace immediately ran to the backside of the barn so that anyone looking out to see 'what was Scruffy's problem' would not see Grace.

Then Grace reached into her bag and quickly altered the dog's attitude toward her by placing peanut butter on the bread and feeding him. Scruffy pretended to be "standoffish" for about thirty seconds and then he accepted the hearty treats and Grace's pats on the head. In only a matter of moments the dog had forgiven Grace and could no longer recall what the problem had been.

Grace had to stop herself from giving Scruffy so much that she would have no supplies left, for she did not yet have a good food supply plan. She also wanted to reenter the cellar before Matt might come home for lunch; so she half hid behind the dog, and they wobbled their way over to the basement door. Here Grace patted him again and left him outside. She crawled into the chimney room and sighed in despair; so much effort, time and money and now she had very little left to show for it. Well, at least she could have raisins for supper, they were healthy.

But poor Grace, who did eat handfuls of raisins that night, suffered the consequences that she had been too young to predict. By four a.m. she was making multiple trips out behind the barn to get rid of intense diarrhea. It was a terrible night and Grace lost about all of the nutrition she had consumed that day. She felt weak and dreary by morning and definitely needed rehydration. This was not a great life.

Just before four, the neighbor had given up on spying out into Grace's driveway to try and see her coming to him. He was angry and frustrated but reasoned he would just have to wait; she would be hungry again.

10

DYING TO EAT

After being sick most of night, Grace felt very empty when she awoke around ten. She was also desperate for a shower and fresh clothing. She went to the top of the stairs and listened. Not a sound met her ear. Elena Maria and the baby could both be sleeping or they could be out walking which was their habit at this time. She crept into the kitchen and from counter height knocked a large illustrated cookbook onto the floor. Then she ducked back down the cellar stairs to listen. No one yelled out "Who's there?" or came running to the kitchen. She waited another two minutes and then rushed into the shower. Here she both washed her body and rinsed her clothing using soap on all.

Then naked, she ran up to her parents' bedroom. Her wet clothing was in a towel which she had first used to dry herself. In her mother's section of the closet she found fresh clothing then went to the dresser for clean socks and panties. She took the wet bundle with her to dry out of sight on a rope she had strung up in the chimney area. Grace felt remarkably better but still hadn't found something to eat.

She again listened at the top of the stairs. All quiet, so she entered remembering she had better check the bathroom to be certain nothing looked wet or out of place. Someone had showered there earlier that day so she had that covered pretty well. She peeked out the kitchen window on her way to the refrigerator. There were her mother and the baby just coming up the driveway. She cursed and ran back down the cellar stairs, clean but hungry. Her lunch had to be the last heel of bread in the bread bag from yesterday with a scoop of peanut butter. It was far better than nothing, but she now was left with nothing.

Feeling despondent, and knowing she must be quiet and keep out of the way, Grace curled up for a nap on her straw mat. The problems of the previous night had worn her out and the shower had helped to relax her so she slept well; but when she awoke near dusk she was ravenous. All she could think about was eating if only that disgusting man next door would leave her alone. She certainly couldn't risk going upstairs again today, nor could she take the amount of food which she desired, as her parents were already curious about missing meals. It seemed she would have to go without. Then she remembered that there were some emergency cookies remaining from her first raid on the neighbors' pantry – those would be dinner. She ate them and slept until two a.m.

At this time, after all she had been through; Grace was not fully awake and only just a bit aware of her surroundings and needs. She started to cry, she wanted her mother, and the only mother she had any access to was sleeping right above her. Almost sleepwalking, Grace lowered the attic stairs and climbed up to her parents' bedroom. She entered through the closet, saw that everyone was asleep, baby Mattie beside their bed, and went over to stand beside her mother.

Grace cried softly for a few minutes then gently touched her mother's hand and said in a whisper "I miss you and need you very much. I wish with all my heart that we could talk. I almost made it as your daughter, didn't I?" Then the tears came in a flood and she made haste to get away before she would be noisily sobbing and gasping. She again used the trapdoor stairs as she feared a ruckus would be started if Scruffy should see her.

Grace ensconced herself back in the chimney room and cried herself to sleep. She was really beginning to wonder if she would have been better off to remain dead or dormant. At least she wouldn't have been so lonely. She slept until morning when the family was getting ready for their day. Grace felt better for she had awakened with a plan.

When the house was empty, including Scruffy, Grace went upstairs and fried one egg, placing it on one piece of toast, and thinking that surely this small amount would not be noticed as missing. She put two apples in her pocket, took another box of cookies, for there were several in the cupboard, drank milk from the bottle, and returned the bottle to the refrigerator. She then cleaned up her mess returning everything to its rightful place, and made her way back to the basement.

Her stomach was satisfied for the moment, and she wasn't filled with terror until later. The terror began to rise inside her like smoke from a fire that will destroy all it touches. That smoke reminded her that she would have to fight with her neighbor to gain access to real food again, and that he wanted to hurt her for any morsel she might garner: a thought that frightened her as much as the food compelled her to go over there this evening. She was glad she had taken a butcher knife from upstairs when she started to head down here this last time. Now she admired the knife and tested its weight in her hands.

By dark, and when her household was quiet, Grace was ready to make her move. She carried an empty bag over one arm so that she could carry food home, and had the knife concealed up her sleeve for ready access. She then crouch-walked across the driveway and through the neighbors' side entry, and into their house where she opened the door slowly, looking both left and right hoping to see the horrid dad before he saw her.

Seeing no one she slid along the hall wall heading for the kitchen. Once into the kitchen she planned to carry out her businesses quickly and quietly using only the light from the refrigerator to illuminate her task. She hoped somehow this fellow was napping upstairs in his own bedroom. But she was wrong. When she stepped into the middle of the darkened room to reach for the appliance he stepped right into her side and placed both his hands around her throat. She gasped, but reached immediately up her sleeve for the weapon.

They struggled for a few moments as he was surprised that this little girl would be brave enough to carry a knife. She was quick; too, for she drew blood from his arm, right through his shirt as he tried to hold her arms down to stop her actions. But he was a grown man weighing close to two hundred pounds more than Grace. He used the knife to frighten her more by also cutting her arm so that she would see the color of her own blood and know that he could draw more, and would do so if he needed to in order to get what he wanted.

She nearly passed out in his arms. He dropped the knife and carried her outside so that his family wouldn't be disturbed. Then he touched her everywhere he wanted to, in all the places that were private to her and which should not be available to him. But to his credit, if such a man may be given any credit, he did not take his pants down; he only used his strong, gnarly, hairy hands to offend her little body. When he was finished he actually wondered, based on so much blood, if she would live, so he carried her out behind her own barn to help eliminate himself as a suspect should she not survive.

He didn't realize that Grace had always been half dead on her biological father's side; and that she now had spider and snake venom in her bloodstream. She was stronger than she looked, stronger than he could imagine, and strong enough to look forward to another opportunity to handle him.

But for tonight she was bloody and hurt. Grace was filled with fear and empty of all energy from her loneliness and lack of nutrition. She was also so humiliated and angered by the things that he had done that her rage had overwhelmed her. She lay on the ground in a heap not daring to move or really wanting to live; and the blood began to puddle around her as a crimson reminder that she could perish.

Hours went by and then Scruffy was let out for his morning "toilet". He sniffed the air and knew immediately that there was fresh blood and that it came from Grace. He rushed around behind the barn and went straight to her. He licked her face seeming to ask "Are you alive?" He nudged her trying to get her to stir. She moaned a little and he knew all this was not good. He ran to the backdoor and started tearing at it with his front paws.

Matt stepped outside about to reprimand the dog for being so rough on the door, but then he saw the blood on Scruffy's paws and fur. He said, "What's going on?" and followed the dog out behind the barn for Scruffy was obviously making circles to pull Matt in that direction. When Matt saw the body he was stunned, but when he rolled the girl over to help her breath and so that he could see her face, he could not even speak from shock, but ran for the house to call an ambulance and to get her mother out there.

11

GRACE AMAZING

When Matt rushed into the house Elena Maria overheard him summoning an ambulance to their address and begging them to hurry. He then went to a medicine cabinet and their linen closet where she found him after she set Mattie back in his crib. She had to ask Matt what was happening. He grabbed her hand and said, "You are going to need all your strength and all your composure for what you are about to see, but we must move quickly for her benefit. Above all else remind yourself to protect that baby within you, but show any emotions you need to because we can handle this together." They were running towards the back of the barn while he was saying these things.

Then Matt stopped abruptly, "It is probably best that I tell you right away, to provide you a few more seconds of adjustment time although this won't nearly be enough. Elena Marie, there is a badly hurt child around the corner and it is Grace! Our Grace!"

Elena Maria brought her hand to her mouth to stifle a cry. Then she ran as fast as she could around that corner to the back of the barn. Whether it was her hormones as a pregnant woman, or simply maternal instinct, and the regret she had been feeling over the loss of Grace, Elena Maria did the correct things.

She crouched on the ground next to the wounded child. She took the pieces of gauze and sheets from her husband and began to make a tourniquet and to cover any wound that she could. She spoke soothingly, but with confidence to Grace saying, "Sweetheart, it is mommy. You are hurt but it is going to be alright. Dad and I are so happy to see you, and we will stay with you. The ambulance is coming so that some very smart doctors can make sure you are going to feel better. If you can hear me, Grace, we love you."

Then they heard the ambulance coming and prepared themselves for a difficult explanation of just who this child was. Matt went back in the house and would care for Mattie while Elena Maria rode in the ambulance with Grace. Everything in Elena Maria's head was in such chaos that she thought it was good to be surrounded by paramedics. She kept repeating to herself "Grace is alive, Grace is alive." She almost laughed hysterically, but the thought that they might also again loose Grace wiped the humor right out of her heart.

The paramedics asked the girl's age and date of birth which Elena Maria could answer based on her knowledge of the birth certificate which they had produced to enroll her in school. She knew her name and stated that she and her husband were legally next of kin. Then she said, "The adoption had not had time to occur when Grace died."

The paramedic said "Is that a joke, lady?" And he pointed at Grace.

"No joke," said Elena Maria. "She was dead and buried. She died of multiple spider bites, but somehow she has returned. She must have only appeared to be dead and somehow got out of the grave."

"Okay, okay," repeated the paramedic. "When did she 'return from the dead'?"

"Well I just don't know. This is the first time I have seen her since the day she died. This morning my husband just found her like this out in the back of the barnyard. We have no idea where she has been or who did this to her."

"Okay," said the paramedic. "I think we'll just have you speak with her doctors and the police to cover all bases when we arrive. We're only five minutes out now." And soon they pulled in at Hartford Children's Hospital, and the fight to save Grace's life began in full force.

Unfortunately, by the time Grace got to help she had slipped into a coma. Elena Maria could not sit with her due to COVID restrictions, but both the police and the medical staff wanted to immediately interview Elena Maria. She answered every question that she could and then explained that she had to get home to her baby as she was breastfeeding, but her husband would come right down to the hospital and answer anything that he could. In the meantime, Elena Maria signed off to allow the doctors to run any tests which they felt were needed. Perhaps some test could help answer the question of where Grace had been.

A hospital volunteer drove Elena Maria home as she had arrived by ambulance. Thankfully this volunteer didn't ask too many questions so that the trip to East Apple was pleasant enough. Elena Maria got home before she completely exploded from the fullness of her breasts; she hadn't been able to nurse her baby for several hours. Still, it was a strange trip worrying the entire way back if her dead daughter would make it or not. This must be what going crazy feels like she thought.

She had told Matt via cell phone how things had been going in Hartford. They both knew that Grace's condition was serious. What Elena Maria was waiting to tell Matt in person was equally difficult. Grace's emergency room doctor, with a policewoman present, had gone over the injuries found on her body. There was the laceration to her left arm, which had done so much bleeding, and there were bruises on her face and neck. It appeared that she had been choked for at least a short time. Most significantly her abdomen, thighs, buttocks, and vaginal area were badly bruised and swollen. There were actually hand prints left on her chest so tightly was she grabbed and groped.

The police assured Elena Maria that they had photographed all these marks to use as evidence in court and to help identify the culprit. Elena Maria was sobbing as she heard these descriptions. She had always felt badly for Grace and now she knew that this terrible treatment only conflated the ordeals which poor little Grace had endured. It was unbearable and yet Grace had suffered this on top of so much the police could never know about.

As Matt learned these things he got increasingly angry. "How could this have happened?" He asked out loud, "And who was around to do such a thing?" This question was a piece of a most sinister set of mysteries all revolving around a girl who appeared to be a sweet ten-year-old. Then he headed for the hospital to sit close-by in case Grace needed him, or the police did.

After Elena Maria nursed her baby she carried him into the cellar, with Scruffy tagging along, to see if Grace had by any chance been living there. What she found in the little area at the base of the chimney confirmed her fears. There were crumbs, hay and her best quilt on the cellar floor. And in one corner she found a pail which Grace must have been using as a commode. It was unfortunate that Grace had not been able to empty this chamber pot for a day or two. Elena Maria could not bear to take on this chore, but she knew Matt would do this to assist his pregnant wife and his poor little girl.

Elena Maria had dreamt, only hours before, that Grace had come and stood at her bed and gently touched her arm. Was this true? Did Grace still care about them? And was there actually a chance that Grace could learn to live a healthy life with them, if she was able to live?

12

THE TEAM

Nonna arrived at Matt and Elena Maria's house. She had been held for a time in that twilight world between life and death. Nonna had only fully returned to life when Elena Maria had successfully pleaded with the captain in the portrait to reach deeply into the portal of time and space in order to bring her mother back to life. For the help he gave them, Elena Maria and Matt were asked to raise the captain's daughter, Grace, who had been shunned from mortal life to a twilight of her own.

The captain had regretted having to truncate the child's life, but she had been a great danger to the family to whom she was born. He made the decision when Grace was threatening the lives of their other children and had killed their pets. The captain had to act to save those children but then had hoped Grace would behave when she returned one hundred and thirty years later to live with Elena Maria and Matt.

This too, nearly ended in tragedy, when Grace repeated cruel acts to animals and nearly fed her baby brother to the spiders. But as the reader knows, Grace was yet again revived from this death caused by spider bites, as her slumber was biologically linked to a state of dormancy common in these spiders, and one which she overcame following a bite by a copperhead snake. Grace was alive, but the DNA the medical facility would discover and the serum in her blood stream, placed the medical team in a position of not knowing how to classify this little girl.

The doctors had good news to give the family, as Grace would live, but they also wanted to explain some unusual findings. When Elena Maria, her mother (Nonna) and Matt attended the meeting with the doctors they were shocked to learn about her serum. Yet, they knew something as unexpected as the return of the dinosaurs could be anticipated when it came to any explanation concerning Grace. So now they heard it from the experts; half of Grace's DNA had been provided by a corpse and her blood was comparable to reptile and arachnid specimens. Further, if the doctors were to believe their patient, she claimed to have been dead at least two times prior to this coma.

Fortunately, no one wanted publicity and Grace appeared to be a sweet child who only engendered sympathy and concern from the staff. The doctors were planning to release her from the hospital as soon as a few more tests could be completed, but the family had some special requests. Matt, Elena Maria and Nonna all believed the child had to have certain impulses controlled with medication or surgery before they could comfortably have her at home.

The medical team called in Dr. Edith at Elena Maria's request. Dr. Edith had discussed Grace in the past when she was being treated by Dr. April, her psychologist; they hoped some of that information would help in choosing a medication to keep Grace more level and less volatile. The family would be happy to have Grace back if she could just function without endangering anyone or herself. Of course the last time Dr. Edith reviewed Grace's case she did not have the two types of venom as part of her blood serum. Doctors and family alike wondered how this good psychiatrist would manage such an unusual case.

Grace was invited to the final medical consultation so that she could be involved as a member of the team making decisions for her future. She listened as her parents explained her strange history to the team leaving out what they felt they must. How could they say that she had been dead just before she arrived at their house the first time? Or how could they explain that she was actually something close to one hundred and forty years old? Of course they said more than they usually did since everyone at the table was aware of her blood work which was so alien that she might have been an extraterrestrial.

The doctors then reviewed this amazing chemistry of Grace's and what it might or might not mean: there were no comparable cases on which to base their conclusions; it was all guess work – a human with all that venom in her blood! Finally, the psychiatrist offered her opinion on which anti-psychotics and antidepressants might work best for Grace. She thought a combination of drugs would be required to help so complex a problem, it was sort of a medical cocktail that Grace was being advised to take.

For her part, Grace was most agreeable. She was willing to take any medication they prescribed that would allow her to function in the world again; she dreamed of sleeping in her old bed, taking a shower whenever she wished and eating meals with her family. So with very little persuasion, Grace was discharged to her parents after receiving another shot in the arm and knowing that her parents were picking up pills for her at the pharmacy.

As they were driving into the yard Grace did inquire as to any progress the police might have made getting the man who had hurt her. Matt replied, "You are very young to understand this but many times when a man touches a girl or a woman the way he touched you he releases a fluid which is what we told you about when you asked us where babies come from. This fluid is not only important to fertilize the mother's egg, but it also important in identifying the man. Because whoever attacked you did not leave this fluid behind, which would provide DNA evidence, the police are looking for other evidence. For example the hand marks he left on your body give them some idea of his size and they are trying to isolate his footprints from those your mother and I left at the scene."

"And Scruffy too," Grace interrupted?

"Yes, and Scruffy too," said Matt

"But," said Grace, "I know who did it. It was the dad from next door. You know, the father of Katie and Stephen and their big sister. He was offering food to me if I let him touch me. I did once and then the second time I was there, and he was putting his stupid hands all over me, I decided to attack him. That's when I pulled out the knife, but he was so big and fat he could just push me down and do anything he wanted and he wanted to touch me where he should not. I couldn't stop him and then I was bleeding and he dumped me outside. I think he wanted me to die so I didn't die, not this time, I decided to live and I can get him later if the police can't!"

"Well," said Elena Maria, "did you tell any of this to the policemen because I'd like to know what they said. We didn't hear any of this from them."

"They said I had better be careful of who I accused. That Mr. Jennings was an important man and that he had a lovely family and that I was known for being a trouble-maker so I had just better watch what I said unless there was some evidence. One of them was nice to me but not the one who acted all in charge."

"Good lord," said Elena Maria, "they had all seemed so concerned and kind when Grace was first hospitalized, what a turn of events!"

"Maybe," said Grace, "that was when they all thought I was going to die and before I told them it was their precious Mr. Jennings. I didn't know those kids had such an important dad."

"You listen to us," said Matt, "we don't care if he is the King of England, we will not let him get away with this, and we will deal with the policeman who said this to you. We love you, and it is our job to protect you. Now Scruffy will sleep next to your bed and watch over you, and we will check-in every little while. You just sleep and let us older people decide what to do."

And they kissed Grace good night.

13

WHO ARE THE JENNINGS

The Jennings had been looking for a house as they sought to flee the city during the early stages of the Pandemic. The students who had been renting the house next door to Elena Maria and Matt moved out just as the COVID virus broke in the news. The students were prompted to leave for two reasons; first, their rental home was linked to the violent man who lived part-time in the woods behind them and had been "haunting" them and the neighbors; and the University started doing remote learning so they really didn't need to pay rent.

For Robert Jennings there was a bit more to the story of his family's quick move than simply fleeing to safety. Robert Jennings was not the pillar of respectability he might appear to be. Oh, on the surface he had a good job as an engineer and a manager, but within his company he was not so much feared as he was loathed, especially by the women. Even though there were laws on the books to guide managers against sexual harassment of their employees, some managers thought that they were clever enough, or powerful enough, or appealing enough, to get away with anything they chose to do with, or to, the women 'underneath' them. This feeling of "too special for the restrictions" may help explain why so many politicians and television personalities get into trouble with sexual harassment; they think the women around them are just yearning for their attentions.

Robert Jennings was one of these fellows. He kept his family's' photograph prominently displayed on his desk as though it were able to shield him from suspicion as a womanizer and a lecher, but it did not slow down his lusty, slimy, actions. If he called a woman into his office she had better be prepared to rebuff his advances with good humor or to give in to them; he could damage careers by reporting that a subordinate had an attitude problem and he could do 'favors' for those who were friendly – very friendly.

One such case involved a young woman in her first position out of college. He started by complimenting Pat on her apparel and then her hairstyle. She was obviously unprepared for these remarks made by her male boss and would flush bright red like a Macy's Santa Claus each time he gave her a "compliment." Then he went a little further and would say, implying this is just between us, that he wished all his staff demonstrated her professional style and was as adept at following orders; that he might have to rearrange his promotional grid to skip over a few people; then he invited her to lunch.

During lunch the compliments continued. He wanted her to know how wonderful he found her thinking, and she would thereafter not wish to disappoint him. But this poor young woman did not know what to do. Pat had no previous corporate experience, but she did have dreams and fantasies of entering the workforce and being immediately recognized for her exceptional strengths. She told herself that this was what was happening, her talent was being recognized. She was going to lunch with the boss not for some clandestine rendezvous, or to set such a thing up, but to discuss how she would be the new blood and strength of the organization as he envisioned it.

The night before their luncheon she spent hours selecting what to wear to work the next day to help clinch the deal of her impending promotion. Naturally she wanted to present herself as professional but also did not want to appear too old school, too stodgy, for the boss's vision of the future. She told herself numerous times that this was not a date but a significant business meeting.

When she arrived early for work in the morning, because she could not sleep and because she was trying to continue enhancing her value in his eyes, she dared not glance toward his office but strode proudly into her own. Within five minutes he had flashed her an interoffice memo stating; you look terrific, can't wait to see you at lunch. She blushed as she read it but secretly suspected she was truly on track for better things.

At lunch Pat was treated like a queen, anything she wanted from the menu was fine. He asked her questions about herself and appeared to hang on every word. Getting to know her was apparently a meaningful opportunity for him. She began to feel more drawn to him; perhaps a quick affair wouldn't be out of the question since they were so drawn to each other.

And then he popped the question: would it be alright if they worked late together the following evening? He wanted to be sure she understood his philosophy before making a bigger commitment. By now she was willing to be molded into whatever he wanted her to be, and if a sex goddess was part of that role she was eager to please. She thought she might be falling in love; she wondered if his marriage was falling apart and he badly needed her attentions. Of course that was it, she surmised, one read about it all the time.

That evening, after the office was quiet, he came to her door and asked her to join him for a discussion. There was a bottle of bourbon on his desk and two glasses. She told him that she had never had bourbon, but he assured her that this was a very smooth and expensive bottle that she was definitely going to like. Then, to further reassure her, he also added ice. She couldn't refuse with all the considerations he was obviously taking, and drinking bourbon was no doubt a corporate rite of passage.

But drinking smooth alcohol, especially when it went down easily, was not necessarily the ideal way for one to learn how to deal with the substance. She didn't object to the first few sips although the heat of the alcohol was surprising to her, but when he poured more into the glass she expressed her concern of quickly becoming drunk. He countered with, "Just relax and loosen up, have some fun, we will be partners through many difficult deals and this will keep us calm. Besides, no one else is here tonight and I've already sent out for Chinese so you'll have food to help absorb anything that's too much for you."

So she drank some more hoping to be seen as a good sport and to clinch their bond. But within a few more minutes she found that she had to giggle a little and then, when she just barely moved her head, she was lightheaded and extremely dizzy. He observed this and came around to her side of the desk sitting nearly on top of her. He said he hoped she wouldn't quit just when they could start to have fun and then he kissed her. Not tenderly, or chastely, but as though his life depended on getting his tongue down her throat.

She pulled back a little. "I think we had better slow down," she said. Just then the buzzer sounded and Jennings let the delivery man up, paying for the food which he set on a side table a few feet away.

"Let me bring you a plate," he said. Then he brought the food over and poured her more bourbon. She foolishly reached and took a sip. At this point the smell of the bourbon and the smell of the broccoli and chicken reached her at the same time. It did not feel right on her already queasy stomach and she gagged a little. This was apparently his cue to move in for she was conscious, but helplessly ill.

He acted solicitous, inquiring about how badly she might be feeling which only made it worse. When her coloring looked like the mustard sauce, he insisted on walking her to the ladies room. Her stumbling along the way offered him several opportunities to fondle her under the guise of helping her, and when she was sick into the toilet bowl he clung to her as she heaved and wretched. He was not a gentleman, he was a devil.

But this must have been the highlight of his evening for afterward he made her coffee and let her sleep undisturbed until he insisted on driving her home and telling her he would say she called in sick, no need to show up the next day. Fortunately, she had no car at the office as she had taken a bus that morning perhaps hoping for a ride home.

Two days later, when she returned to the office, she immediately asked to see him. She could not recall much of what had happened that evening, but felt she might have made a fool of herself. She was all apologies, and how may I make it up to you. He was gracious and said he blamed himself for introducing the bourbon into their meeting. Then he very pointedly said she could compensate him by going on a "business trip" with him the next weekend. She wanted to say "no thank you" for it just didn't seem right with him as a married man, etc., but she said "Okay".

They took that trip. He had only booked one room and soon he was filling her head again with compliments and trying to get liquor into her. She succumbed but only after he promised that he loved and admired her and that there were big things ahead for her in the company's future. It was like a honeymoon for him but she was filled with anxiety and doubts.

The doubts were called for as he acted as though he hardly knew her the following Monday. She kept trying to get a moment alone with Jennings, and he kept throwing hurdles in front of her. Finally, by Thursday, she too avoided him and spent most of her time crying behind closed doors.

The following week she watched him escort another young and attractive woman out to lunch. Pat went to the cafeteria for the first time in weeks and intentionally sat with the 'gossip girls'. She let a few words drop about Robert Jennings looking like a lady's man and they jumped right in. She soon learned that he had a girlfriend of the month and had cost several women their jobs if they chose to complain.

Pat didn't complain but she did send an anonymous letter to his wife.

14

JENNINGS AT HOME

The letter to Mrs. Jennings stirred up considerable trouble, as might be imagined. Here she was managing the lives of three small children, day after day, with minimal input from hubby. In point of fact, he frequently came home when the children were already asleep and he reeked of alcohol. Added to this were his frequent weekend business trips, and one might guess that their marriage was already moving closer to the spot by the road where garbage was collected. And then Pat's letter arrived.

Now, Pat wasn't so bold as to sign her name, but she did claim to be speaking for "an unfortunate group of women at Medley, Medley and Johnson." Then she described Robert's smooth talking, alcohol pumping, and general molestation of these poor gals. She implied that the word was he went even further on the special weekends. The Mrs. was ready to raise his voice several octaves; she thought of all the benefits of widowhood; and she certainly started thinking about divorce. But when Robert was confronted with the note he bluffed and cajoled his way through it and practiced some of his greatest charm on his wife, who was love-starved.

They formed a truce which involved Robert pledging fidelity once again, getting home for at least three weekday dinners on average, and cutting his weekends away in half. Naturally he protested as to how this might ruin his career, but the Mrs. held fast. She had read quite a bit in that anonymous letter that rang true for her. He had originally charmed and seduced her with flattery and alcohol, perhaps his method of operation had not varied much over time. She tried not to be disgusted with him for what she saw as his major weakness: he didn't ever feel secure so the only way he could conquer someone was by being bigger, or having an unseen upper hand, or knowing that they were impaired by age, alcohol, or position. Perhaps his maneuvering for power with these women was mistaken for sexual advances she guessed.

Those three youngsters deserved to grow up with an intact family. They also had a very nice apartment in New York not far from the park. She had reasons to ignore his peccadilloes that went beyond simple consideration for her spouse.

But as times changed, and the corporate 'normal' was more in keeping with respecting women, placing women in leadership positions and believing women who accused men of harassing them, Robert began to feel uncomfortable even away from home. He was quoted by a male colleague as saying "Geez, what's a guy got to do to get laid around here anymore?" Apparently he was being turned down and not always with good humor. In fact, to keep his job, he had to agree to work out of a different office for six months. The home office wanted a chance for all parties to "cool down" before allowing him back in. He protected himself by moving his wife away from the area where too many people knew him to be sleazy. He was happy to commute a distance to keep his wife in the dark and the "injured" parties from pressing charges.

Although Mrs. Jennings was initially very resistant to this move, the pandemic fears covered up a lot of Robert's problems by making a grand excuse to leave New York. The Jennings were part of a mass of people wanting to get out of the city. If they were going to be quarantined at least it was good to be in a home where one had space both inside and outside. Country living provided the opportunity to roam the woodland without running into people who were very possibly contagious, so families were very drawn to these settings. Elena Maria and Matt had been warned not to try and sell their place while the deaths in their home were still making the news. But apparently a house that abutted their property was not so stigmatized. So, when the rental house went on the market, the Jennings were first in line to purchase it and moved in almost immediately.

Without a variety of young, needy women routinely coming into his life, Robert Jennings did what he felt any red-blooded male would do; he slowly but steadily started grooming his youngest daughter to give him pleasure. He began by showing her more attention than he gave to anyone else. He combined this with little surprise presents just for her, and she was not to tell her siblings about them. He started helping her study behind closed doors so that they developed an intimacy; then he began massaging her neck and shoulders if he thought she had been studying too much; finally he inched his fingers into places they had absolutely no business being, and would provide no comfort for anyone but himself.

By this time Katie felt very confused. She was young and often lonely, but always felt icky when touched this way. Still, it didn't seem like it would be a good thing to tell on daddy; she knew daddy could get very angry. She was trying to sort this all out at the same time she was beginning to have some problems with the new girl next door who was in her grade. She wondered if this girl somehow knew about her and her father, there was something so unusual about Grace; or maybe she would do well to get advice from her teacher. But in the midst of all these thoughts there was a terrible tragedy and Grace died.

Katie had never had a friend die before and she shut down. She just wouldn't say much to anyone for several weeks after Grace 'went to heaven' as her mother described it. She hadn't liked Grace but that fact added to her feelings of guilt. Could she have wished Grace to death? And, while she felt alone with her feelings which were very mixed up she found that her father was leaving her alone during this strange time. Then one night, weeks later, she found daddy kissing Grace almost inside the refrigerator.

Katie ran back to her room in terror of being seen and of having seen a ghost, but she soon discovered that her father wasn't bothering her, not one little bit, now that he had found Grace. She knew Grace must not have died and had been brought back home. Perhaps her parents had forgiven her for all the awful things she had done. And perhaps they also didn't want the neighbors to know because Grace had hurt them, maybe even tried to kill Stephen. Anyway, Katie didn't want to be the one who told that Grace was back especially as it involved her dad, and he would just starting touching her again if he couldn't touch Grace. That's what he had called it, "touching" and "there is nothing wrong with touching, right Katie," he would always say. So she was quiet.

Then early one morning the ambulance came. The police and the officers knocked on their door to ask if they had heard or seen anything. Katie knew it had to do with Grace, but she stayed quietly in the background. Still, she wondered, if touching was so fine why did her father pretend that he had not seen Grace since her funeral? Why did daddy also have big bandages hidden under his sweater? How had he gotten hurt if he wasn't involved? This was just another lie grownups tell, and the only way to remain safe was to pretend that she knew nothing.

Katie also knew her momma wasn't very happy. Her mom had cried when they had to leave their fancy apartment in New York. Momma knew East Apple because she had an aunt here, but she didn't seem to think that there was much culture out here; she thought the area would stifle her creativity: only small museums, little opera or theater, what a shame for her children she had said. Then she was mad at daddy for quite awhile. She told her aunt that she could only live for the children now; Robert was a lost cause, whatever that meant.

Little did mother know that her husband had not only done harm to the adult women in his office, which she had learned about, but that he had routinely been molesting little Katie and had now been involved in a brutal attack on the girl next door. She still didn't know that Grace was actually alive so she experienced great shock when the police returned to their door to ask more questions and named Grace as the victim!

The officers came into the house and were very polite. They explained that they were only bothering them again because the victim lived next door, and that was how Mrs. Jennings learned that Grace had returned from the grave. Funny, she thought, that girl was so strange I could almost believe she was haunted.

The police also mentioned their gratitude for the donations her husband had been making to the whole community and the fact that he was likely to run for selectman the following November. Barbara Jennings could only smile and thank them for their kindness. She didn't want to say "he can run as long as none of his chickens come home to roost."

15

DEFINITELY NOT DORMANT

I t took Grace a couple of days to fully awaken following the beating. Yes, she had been speaking with people, especially her family, but there was always fuzz in her brain. She wanted to shake her head and snap out of something, but no amount of blinking or cold water splashed on her face, or even slapping her own cheeks, could make her wake up until the morning of the third day. That was when she could not lay in bed any longer.

When her folks walked downstairs for breakfast Grace was sitting at the table and asked, as though it was the most natural thing in the world for your dead daughter to request, "May I have bacon and eggs?"

Matt immediately opened the refrigerator and began removing the ingredients that would be needed. Elena Maria sat down next to Grace and just hugged her with one arm while she held onto the baby with the other. Grace reached back toward her and rubbed the baby's beautiful bald forehead with her own hand. It was a very loving scene, but fraught with so many layers of unanswered questions that

CYNTHIA HERBERT-BRUSCHI ADAMS

it might be seen as the side of a gorge where all the stones above the bottom were striated by thousands of years of glaciers.

Finally, Elena Maria sat up and said, "While dad is cooking for us can you explain one more time how you were able to resurrect yourself, or did your father reach back for you from the portal?"

"I have had no contact with my father; in fact I have avoided the portrait altogether. You will find this so creepy that I hate to tell you, but before all of the Goliath Bird Eating Spiders died or went into dormancy, they came to bring me back from the cemetery. They actually dug me up and I awakened, but realizing I was stuck in a box I went back to sleep. Each time I tried to wake up it was always overwhelmingly dark. Then something happened; the casket may have been dropped, anyway I started to see a glimmer of light in one corner. Then a snake came in and didn't like sharing its hiding place with me. It bit me. Yet, shortly after the bite I started to feel more awake, more alive and then I just found all this strength and forced my way out of the ground. Thank heavens there wasn't much dirt on my coffin there in the cellar, for that is where I awoke, back home here in the cellar."

And Elena Maria filled in "And from then on you tried to take care of yourself here in the house without us knowing that you were back?"

"Yes," replied Grace. "That is how I got mixed up with Mr. Jennings when I was trying to get enough food to eat without you and dad figuring out someone was again scavenging food from you. But he caught me and said not to worry; he would feed me as long as I didn't tell about the way he was touching me. If I kept quiet I could eat. Only I wanted to have it both ways. I wanted to still take food from their refrigerator but miss running into him. Only somehow he was always alert to when I would come and go. And his

72

hands were always touching me in naughty places until he got really angry with me and decided to hit me, over and over again. Still, it was probably my fault; I had brought a knife to make him leave me alone only he used it on me. Then we were both stabbed, but I was bleeding a lot more than he was, and he left me to bleed all night. Like my own father, he just wanted me dead!" And she sobbed.

Matt spoke up, "Well now I am your father, and if you can just stop dangerous behaviors we will protect you and treat you with love."

"But," she said, "You were happy enough when the spiders killed me this last time, you weren't in mourning."

"We were very mixed up," he replied. "We had become very fearful of what you might do to the baby, but we did not want to lose you. I guess you know the feeling, to want it both ways; safety for the baby and the neighbors, but our beautiful daughter at home. And the doctors think we can have that healthy behavior this time with the right medications."

They had breakfast, and then after eating Matt explained he was going to the State Police barracks to see what could be done about Mr. Jennings because he had to pay for the harm he had done to Grace and he had to be stopped from hurting other girls. The police told him a school counselor had already interviewed the Jennings children. They had reported that Grace was always a trouble maker. That this time she was only stealing food, but that other times she had hurt their brother and they blamed her for the giant spider that had killed their parakeet.

The officer concluded that these children did not find any fault with their father and that they were all afraid of Grace. Also that it was Grace's word against Mr. Jennings' as there was no proof that he had hurt her; the stab wounds were made with a knife from the Nelson's own household. And there was no DNA evidence which would have indicated a sexual assault.

Matt said "Perhaps Jennings had kept the "DNA" to himself, but Grace had not stabbed herself." He also indicated that "the paramedics had taken photographs of the hand marks on Grace's poor body. Did they think Grace had put on a man's gloves and slapped herself? And what about leaving a ten-year-old child who was badly bleeding? Wasn't that attempted murder?"

The officer said, "Settle down, Dr. Nelson. Of course you are upset; after all you had just buried this girl, but don't try and put all your problems on a neighbor."

This remark infuriated Matt. He said, "I never thought it would be necessary to take matters into our own hands in such an obvious case. But, if the police will do nothing then we will act to protect our own child!" And with that he rapidly exited the barracks.

Thankfully, Matt had calmed down some by the time he reached home. He had already decided he must cancel his classes that day in order to make sense of what he and his family were up against. They had to have a way to handle this man for what he had done to Grace and to protect her in the future.

Matt went inside and spoke privately with Elena Maria to explain how irrational the police seemed to be and how they must take steps to protect Grace. Elena Maria added, "And to bring Jennings to justice!"

"Well, we certainly hope so," said Matt.

Then both parents tried to explain to Grace how the police did not have enough evidence to go after Mr. Jennings just yet. While her eyes looked horrified, she seemed to accept what they were saying especially since they insisted that there was still hope of getting him arrested.

Matt and Elena Maria also called their attorney and attempted to get her read on this. Just what could they, as private citizens, get away with legally speaking? Neither she nor her partners were very encouraging, in fact they warned them that anything they tried might get them in trouble. Grace over heard enough of this to be despondent; but only for awhile.

Then a feeling came over Grace that she was starting to think of as her inner serpent: it came over her when she broke out of the coffin; when she pulled the knife on Mr. Jennings it had been there too, but she had mistakenly held it back; now she had to muster all of its strength to know she could overcome this large man, even by sheer force if she had to!

16

METAMORPHOSIS

Grace concentrated on her inner strength. She needed to be brave just to survive this transition from dead, or hiding, to living and interacting. There were many barriers for a girl who had just left a coffin, and was now facing starting school. Many of the other children had attended her funeral and they could not easily accept her return to life. Schools had just reopened in full in Connecticut after being on Zoom or hybrid programs during the height of the COVID pandemic. In some ways it might seem that Grace had not missed too many lessons, but the impact of her "returning from the dead" could not be discounted both on Grace and the other kids.

Even without being in the classroom, Grace was harangued by other children after they learned about her miraculous return to life. There were 'drive-bys' at the Nelsons' house night and day; kids who wanted to see the 'Spirit Child' or the 'Ghost of Grace' made pests of themselves not only with the things they yelled, but they also tossed rotten fruit on the front yard. Their point, apparently, was that Grace must like food that was ready for the compost just like she was: cruel and hurtful messages which Grace had to take in and try her best to shake off.

These occurrences certainly confirmed that Grace was not going to be welcome back at school. The Nelsons and Grace agreed that she would be happy with a tutor who would come into the home. This was a good solution but not entirely satisfactory for a child who was terribly lonely. Grace needed at least one confidant in addition to her parents and grandparents; Grace needed a friend.

Naturally, the easiest solution would have been if Katie's mother would give Grace another chance to prove she was capable of playing nicely, but the accusation of Mr. Jennings, coupled with the oddness of Grace's story, simply made that situation unlikely. Grace coped by walking Scruffy, playing ball with him, and sometimes even dressing him up in some of her old clothing.

It happened that one day Katie had stayed home from school with an upset stomach, but partway through the morning she had started to feel better and was leaning on the back of a couch looking out her window at Grace playing with the dog. Katie knew her father had done the crime because she had seen them once. She also knew he had done the crime because he had molested her – many, many times. She hated her father, but had not been honest with the police regarding her dad as she greatly feared him.

Katie thought about Grace all the time: how horrible it must have been to wake up in the coffin, what panic she must have experienced when she didn't know how to get food and how disgusting it must have been for her to let this fat, hairy man maul her. She wished she could talk to Grace as they had a lot in common with extreme loneliness and hatred for her father.

She was concentrating on these feelings so intently that she didn't see Grace walk up toward her window but still remaining on her own property, pull down her mask and give Katie a most inviting grin. Katie immediately withdrew from the window, but the moment she pulled away from Grace she regretted it. After a few seconds she stood up and looked back. Grace was still standing there as though expecting this response from Katie. Then Katie held up one finger seeming to signal 'one minute' and within that moment she popped out the side door and was only a few feet away from Grace.

Both girls couldn't help but giggle; they were each so ecstatic to behold the other. They laughed until the tears came, then Grace said, "I'd probably better not come over to your house," so Katie crossed over the property line and was standing next to Grace when Elena Maria looked out the window.

Quickly, Elena Maria joined the girls to ascertain the nature of this rendezvous, which she was then thrilled to discover seemed cordial. Katie said that her mother wasn't home and she wasn't to leave her house so Elena Maria brought out two folding chairs and told the girls to each sit in their own yards for as long as they both felt comfortable. She almost added "And don't discuss the case" but decided to stay out of that since they were each so young. She did add that she would be back outside in a little bit and would bring them some Cokes. Then she hurried in so that she could hear Mattie if he cried.

As soon as Elena Maria was out of ear shot Katie said she had something to tell Grace. As she spoke the tears began to roll down her cheeks, then she said, "I know you have been telling the truth because my father has also been a molester at home, and I'm pretty sure he got into trouble at work for the same thing. I know my mother has been really angry with him. I didn't dare tell the police because I thought he would murder me just like he almost killed you!"

Grace sat for a moment with her mouth open wide. She had awakened that morning feeling isolated and alone; like the sun wouldn't shine on her, just everyone else, a worthless sense. Now, within a few minutes of starting to play in the yard with Scruffy, she had a friend again AND someone who absolutely believed her. Then an awful thought crossed her mind and she had to ask Katie.

"What," she said, "has he done since my story was told in the papers? Has he done anything to hurt you? When Katie failed to respond she added "Is he touching you again?"

Katie's tears overflowed her eyes and ran down her cheeks falling on her lap. She answered in a quavering voice, "He does things to me almost every night. I hate him, I really hate him."

Grace said, "I wasn't going to tell this to anyone, not even my mother, because she will worry too much and maybe even put me on more medication, but I am changing."

"What do you mean, changing, are you getting your period like my big sister does?"

"No," responded Grace, "it is different. I feel my brain telling me I can change my whole body and be strong and fight off anyone, even a man. I just have to want it to happen with all my heart and my legs will seal together and be covered with one skin; my arms will become long in front of me, also one skin. And my tongue will twitch out fast and pointed between fangs. I can become a snake like the one that gave me strength and set me free from the coffin."

"Are you sure?" asked Katie, totally mesmerized by this suggestion.

"Just about positive," said Grace, "but I haven't dared to try it out yet. I think I may need to be provoked, you know, upset about something, to make it work. You said your father bothers you every night? Well can you lead him out to this little garden area if he comes for you tonight? I'll wait for you here in the bushes and if he comes out touching you just say 'Stop daddy, stop' and I'll change into the serpent, I swear I can change. That way we'll be each other's witnesses and protect each other."

"I think I can do that," said Katie, "but promise me that you'll be here because I'll be counting on it."

"Sure thing," said Grace, "sure thing."

Then Elena Maria brought out soda and crackers for them to enjoy as a little picnic. She asked if everything was alright and both girls said great. There were no tears showing.

17

BLOOD SISTERS

G race was ecstatic to have a friend. She wondered if the medications had helped her to be more aware of other people and to possibly be considerate of their needs, or had she found Katie at the right time in her life when they both had similar problems to be addressed? Whatever the answer she felt like a different girl just knowing there was someone she could talk with about what really worried her.

Elena Maria could also see the change in her daughter; both girls had asked her to join them when she had delivered the snacks, and both had chatted very naturally about kids they used to be in class with, almost as though a mother wasn't sitting with them. She knew this wouldn't last, and that the girls should have their privacy and develop some of their likes and dislikes as separate from a parent, but it meant something to Elena Maria that they had simply asked her to stay. Of course, within five minutes she was too anxious about the sleeping baby to remain in the garden, but the kindness had been extended and well received.

Then Grace came in and she busied herself helping to set the table and even changed a diaper. When Matt arrived home he received the news of her having a pleasant time with Katie as quite an accomplishment. All this praise and warmth began to worry Grace. What would her parents think if they knew of her plans for later that night? Did they still expect that the best course of action for Mr. Jennings was through the authorities or the law? Would Grace be considered a troublemaker as in the old days if she used violence against this neighbor? Would they consider Grace a failure and give up on her if she fought back? Did they understand that Katie's life was a horror knowing each night she would be pushed, poked, fondled and prodded by her dad until she wanted to disappear? Some nights Katie had said that she felt so badly she practically scalded herself in the shower; she just didn't know how to feel clean anymore.

Katie had thought about telling her mother, but she remembered all the tears her mom had shed when she received a letter from a woman at her dad's office declaring that her father had done bad things at work. She felt she must protect her mother from any more pain. If her mother had been upset because dad was touching a grown-up lady in a disgusting way, just think how outraged she would be to know dad was doing that same stuff to his youngest daughter. She could not bear to provoke this pain in her poor mom. But now she had Grace.

Then Katie went down for dinner with her mother, sister and little brother. Dad was often late for meals due to Zoom meetings, conference calls, or day trips for business. Dinner was always more pleasant if he were not present; no anger and tension at the table, no fear of being hit if you said the wrong thing, or watching your sibling being humiliated and cowed by one of dad's tirades, and, of course, when dad finished his rage on one, it was likely to spill right over onto you within moments. This fear of being the next to get hit sometimes led to involuntary grimaces or eye shifts and that was all dad needed for permission to beginning hitting again.

Katie wondered if her poor little brother had been so wounded since the beginning of his life that he almost had a death wish. When dad was acting out on one of the girls he would run at and push his father and tell him not to hit them. Then his dad would gladly trade whacking one for another and beat on this poor little kid. With her baby being hit, their mother would try to intervene and more than likely be shoved to the side, or worse. Those were the worst nights, when everyone but dad would end up crying and not eating.

The only time dad wasn't mean to Katie, in the angry way, was when he was working on her to get her comfortable to accept his very private touches. She knew that she was never "comfortable" with his pokes and squeezes, but sometimes she just couldn't fight him; there was little fight left in her.

Tonight mom said that dad had just called and would not be coming home for supper. He said that he was having dinner at a client's house and that they should not wait up for him, maybe he would catch up with everybody at breakfast. "Wow," blurted out to her sister, "A night off!" Her mother said to "hush now", but she looked as pleased as the kids all acted.

Katie had to get to the phone. Although she was considered too young to have her own cell there was an extension line in the upstairs hallway which still afforded her some privacy. She asked Mrs. Nelson if Grace could come to the phone. She later learned that there was a slight hesitation; as the family had just sat down to eat, but Mrs. Nelson was so pleased that Grace had a friend who would call her that she wanted to make it easy and allowed Grace to interrupt her dinner.

When Grace returned to the table her mother asked what Katie had wanted. Grace replied, "Oh, we had talked about trying to catch some peepers tonight because they have been so noisy the last few days, but her mom said she hadn't finished enough homework so maybe tomorrow night," hastily adding, "If that's okay with you?" And with that, Grace experienced great relief and went back to her lasagna.

Later she called Katie back just to make certain that she was ok. Grace admitted that she would be prepared for the next night but was glad that Katie did not have to worry that night. Katie agreed that she was happy not to see her dad that night, but that she had been hoping to get things over with.

From Grace's point of view the following night came too fast. Her stomach had been rebellious all day. First it craved food as though eating could mask the tension and soothe the inner self, but when she had something delicious in front of her it started to taste dusty after two bites. She would be full after eating nearly nothing and then starving again soon after. Her mom asked if she was alright and she said yes, just growing pains she guessed as Grace had not grown in years having been preserved by the portal to float in time. It was true; Grace would now have to deal with the human condition as well as all the matters of day-to-day life which for Grace were anything but normal.

Evening arrived and Grace wanted the family to see her as relaxed even though she was quite anxious. She consumed most of her meal and made conversation with them. She answered that, yes, she would be out hunting peepers near the edge of the swamp with Katie and would certainly wear her bug repellant. She promised not to be out too late, and then the gathering broke up and Grace prepared to go hide near Katie's garden. This was very likely the night she must challenge Mr. Jennings to help save Katie.

Grace was plenty nervous because Katie was counting on her and because she believed that Mr. Jennings deserved a severe punishment; she just hoped however it turned out that she would not be seen as crazy or too cruel. She did not want to lose her family's love and respect.

Grace had been crouched in the shrubs for about fifteen minutes when she heard the Jennings' side door open with a bang and saw Katie stumble out being pushed ahead by her dad. He was speaking in a low voice saying something about just how much Katie meant to him and how she must know that she was his favorite and the only one who really knew him and could understand him. Wouldn't she please play nice with her daddy?

It looked like she must have been dressed for bed when he had begun things with her on this night for her hair appeared damp and she was wearing pajamas with little teddy bears on them. He quickly pushed her up against the side of the house and as he stood towering above her he reached his left hand down into her pants and pulled her head back so that he could kiss her. Her neck was under pressure as it was tipped back so far that it gave her no choice but to comply and open her mouth. When he finally pulled away she was fighting to breathe and turning from him. She said the important words, "Stop daddy, Stop!"

With that Grace felt an overwhelming burst of adrenaline and almost a buzzing or a vibrating of her skin. Her clothing fell from her body and a strength like a thousand freight trains coursed through her veins. She looked down at herself and was stunned to see not her copperhead venom taking charge but the cause of her dormancy had taken over and she was the most enormous Giant Goliath Bird Eating Spider!

Grace knew that this creature, who was she, could handle anything. She marched over to the struggling couple and jumped on Mr. Jennings back as he continued to fondle his little daughter. This unexpected pressure on him made him release the child who ran for the house with her hands over her mouth. As Grace was getting ready to restrain Mr. Jennings in a cocoon for future digestion or just captivity, he grabbed a large rock from the ground and swung his arm around striking the spider on one of the arms that was gripping him.

18

JUGULAR

"Ugh," thought the spider as she fought back pain. She had not anticipated that her prey would fight back. Instead of wrapping him up so that she and Katie might decide his fate later, she simply reacted to being wounded. She bit the man with so much power that her mouth felt as though it had become a car crusher in a junkyard and would be flattening him into tinfoil. But, it was only a bite, although she did land it on his jugular.

What Mr. Jennings saw was two hideous black eyes which showed no sign of recognition or empathy; the eyes just saw him well enough to aim its two piercing pincer-like fangs into the side of his neck. And it was a very big spider; perhaps the shock of it jumping on him, or the fright of such an attack, coupled with his bloodstream being infused from the sting, caused him to pass out suddenly hitting his head on a flagstone in the walkway.

Grace did not know her own strength in this new body. Since she had not yet decided if he should be killed, and what that would mean to her, it is likely just as well that the dose was not lethal; soon Mrs. Jennings would help him into the house. His problems were, however, not over. His wife, who typically went to bed early, had been awakened by her youngest daughter who was sobbing that "A monster got daddy!" When Mrs. Jennings prodded Katie just a little, she soon learned that her husband had been trying some 'funny business' with the child. She never did connect the monster to her husband's bad deeds or to Grace, but she understood enough that, shall we say, she kicked a man while he was down before helping him inside.

Grace had survived the blow to one of her legs/arms; she wasn't sure what to call it, and reacted by curling up into a ball until the pain went away and the person who had struck her was dragged in like a dead ant to hide in its nest. Then she extended all her parts and felt only slightly off balance and inconvenienced by the wound. In the dark she made her way through the thicket and across the lawn to her home.

Now the big question was how to get back to her bedroom without disturbing the family. Before she left for this adventure, she had constructed a sort of dummy in her bed so that if her parents peaked in they would think Grace was asleep. The trick was how to be in that bed by morning with this hurt appendage deterring progress. But as she crouched on the ground outside she remembered that she was extremely strong. She still had many good legs left so she placed three in front of her on the side of the house, knowing that one was weak, and allowed the back legs to propel her up the side of her house until she reached her bedroom window. Here she waited to catch her breath and then worked two of her pronged appendages under the window. The window was never locked as this was the second floor, so she leveraged her backside and with an easy upward motion the window was open and the Grace-nid was inside.

Her drop was light, not noisy, but as she rested on the floor her transformation began. The legs became shorter until they were reabsorbed by her body; then the facial features metamorphosized from arachnid to human. By the time Grace rolled over she was Grace again. There was an ugly, painful, bruise on her right shoulder, but nothing was broken and this injury could easily be concealed with a long-sleeved shirt. She hastily unmade the dummy putting its parts away and then she curled up in bed. Grace hoped Katie was okay, and as she was trying to decide what her wishes were for Mr. Jennings' condition, she fell sound asleep. Apparently spiders do not have much of a conscience.

The next morning her parents had to call her twice for breakfast as it required a great deal of effort to wake-up; this transformation business must demand a great deal of energy. Grace was extremely hungry going through not only the eggs and bacon which had been prepared for her, but an additional six pieces of toast. "You must be growing," her father said, and so she must be as she continued to live as a mortal; only Grace knew some aspects of her were not normal.

She and Katie met out in the yard as soon as the day was really underway. Katie was so glad that Grace was not badly hurt and wanted to thank Grace. Grace was equally concerned about Katie. Did she think her father would bother her tonight? Had he taken his anger out on her? How was her mother?

Katie said she wasn't sure what her dad would do, but her mother seemed to 'be on to him' as though she knew he was doing bad things to her and had warned him to stop it. "Of course," Katie added, "he's been told to behave before, and he doesn't seem to know how to control himself." It sounded as though this child could easily be an adult describing a child, rather than her own father. Then she added, "I'll probably be okay tonight, he'll be too scared to try anything."

"Okay," said Grace, "I probably need to give myself a little time to recover and don't want my parents to be suspicious if my behavior seems off."

Unfortunately, two things happened that night. Long after the rest of the community seemed to be sleeping Mr. Jennings arose to just check in on his youngest daughter. When he looked into her room he did not see her there so he checked the other kids' rooms and found her, curled up in the bottom of her little brother's bed. For whatever reason this seemed to infuriate him; perhaps he was jealous that she sought out her brother, but rejected him, her father; or that she was hiding from him. He wanted to make certain that she knew he was the boss even if her mother appeared to be some of the time. He wanted her to know that he could do what he wanted and when he wanted, and no damn spider-monster was going to get the better of him – ever!

Whatever his thinking was, he entered the little boy's room, and placing his hand over Katie's face, removed her from the bed. Naturally, she awoke, and he whispered crossly into her ear, no longer pretending to be sweet with her, that he would show her that he was the boss. Then he took her out to their garage where he assaulted her so badly that even he panicked. He could see that these marks would remain, that certainly his wife and even the authorities would have evidence against him. He thought about his budding political career and how that would be lost since the accusations by that girl next door still hung over him and that adding his daughter's bruises to public information would finishe him off; no selectman or the dreams he had of going further.

He wasn't thinking clearly, but the only remedy that popped out at him, meant he would have to act fast. Before he could change his mind he grabbed a few things from the house, threw Katie into the trunk of his car, and drove rapidly out of town. When he came to a gravel quarry about fifteen minutes from home he tied her, poured vegetable oil on her, and left her for the animals. Fox, coyotes, and even wolves frequented this wooded village. There were also sightings of bear and bobcats every few months, so he felt certain that he could leave a helpless child tied-up and beaten with no worry that she would make it through the night. Somehow he could not actually pull the trigger to mortally wound his youngest daughter but he could "let nature take its course" as he told himself. With a jerky look of farewell, he turned his car around and headed for home.

As he sped back to East Apple he started to chuckle. Pretty soon this chuckle turned to laughter and then uproarious laughter: when the police peppered him with questions about his child's disappearance he would slowly and reluctantly implicate Grace. After all she and Katie had trouble in the past and Grace was well known to the authorities for her history of mental derangement. Why she was even thought to have had something to do with the spider that had killed Katie's parakeet; she'd make the perfect patsy, he'd be home free. Now he'd just crawl into bed and let his wife wake him with the news come morning.

19

OH WHERE OH WHERE

The police were all over East Apple by the time Grace was awakened in the morning. They had knocked on the side door of her house and spoken with Elena Maria who was just starting coffee after having finished feeding Mattie. They reported that little Katie next door had been kidnapped during the night while she slept in her own bed. It was a horrible crime. Had they seen or heard anything out of the ordinary? When was the last time they had seen Katie Jennings, and how had she seemed? Where was their daughter Grace and where had she been last night? If they heard anything of interest or thought of anything that could be relevant would they please call Officer Stuart at the following number, and they handed Elena Maria a card. Then they added: "Please don't leave the area until this case is resolved, or we find the missing child."

Elena Maria was in shock. How could this happen in beautiful bucolic East Apple where the last crime committed was probably when an apple pie cooling on a window sill was stolen by a teenager who was drawn to the aroma? These things just didn't happen. Then she had to recall that her own daughter had been abused by the father of the little girl who was missing. That was a serious crime, and who knew if he might have something to do with his own child's disappearance? Had the police thought of that? She rushed to speak with Matt, and together they would tell Grace the terrible news.

Grace was devastated by the thought of something bad having happened to Katie. She immediately stated to her parents that she blamed Mr. Jennings because of what he had done to her and because she knew he was molesting Katie. Elena Maria assured Grace that she would tell the detective who had been there about Mr. Jennings. The police should know that his own little girl had been afraid of him. It being a Sunday, and under these terrible circumstances, Matt, Elena Maria and Grace would all start hunting for Katie.

The detective advised the family to look for Katie close to home. If she had wandered off, or been carried away, it was likely she wouldn't have gotten too far. Matt said that he and Grace should take Scruffy out with them and walk through their backyard close to where it abutted the Jennings' property. Grace changed her clothing in two minutes and off they went. They started at the Jennings' backdoor, where Scruffy was very interested in some scent, and continued out to the woods from there. Scruffy was soon more interested in squirrels and disinterested in anything Grace gave him to smell that had been touched by Katie.

Matt said that might mean they had gone the wrong way; they should go back to where Scruffy had been excited and lead him in the opposite direction from the woods. By so doing they ended up nearly making a circle around the Jennings' home until they were practically underneath it pointed at the garage. Here Scruffy started pawing and whining for attention; he wanted to get into the garage. Matt called the officer from his cell and was told that the police had already been in the garage and had not found the child. That they, the Nelsons, could search outside only and if they did more than that they would interfere with the police and quite possibly destroy evidence.

Grace heard her father apologize to the officer and say that they would leave the immediate area. Then they went home to check-in with Elena Marie and to think about where a criminal might take the child if all they wanted to do was to get rid of the girl and return home. "You mean how Mr. Jennings might have acted?" asked Grace.

"Yes," said her dad. They were thinking the same way about this man.

Elena Maria put Mattie into his stroller. She decided that the smartest way they could help would be to walk along Cemetery Hill Road wherever it abutted woodland where a child might be lost.

Grace and her father drove around somewhat aimlessly. Occasionally, they would let Scruffy out on his leash to see what reaction he might have to a pull off, or a stretch of woods, or a shack by the side of the road, but they got nothing. They just kept hoping that the hundreds of other volunteers who were heading out right after church would have better luck than they.

Their hearts felt like throbbing Jell-O when they left their searching duty to report in at home. They pulled into their driveway as two police officers were arriving. The officers were apologizing for what they must do, as Grace was so young and had been through so much, but that they had to take Grace in for questioning. Naturally a parent must be present and they were welcome to contact a lawyer. It seemed Mr. Jennings was saying that the family suspected Grace for Grace was known to dislike Katie and lived so close-by she could easily have committed the crime and slipped back home undetected.

Meanwhile, a mother and son were pulling into the entrance of the gravel quarry where Jennings had left Katie. They were driving a fancy "Woody", this one from the early 1950s. It was a station wagon that had actual wood paneling on its sides making it a most unusual and very heavy automobile. They were headed to Massachusetts after attending a car show in Rhode Island for vintage automobiles and had decided to use this spot for a picnic and a rest stop since there were not many other choices for them between Rhode Island and home.

Soon after they set up their little folding table and chairs, the son went around to the back of the Woody to retrieve the picnic basket. He thought he could hear a faint moaning and mentioned it to his mother. She said "Well, go on and have a look around that shed, maybe a critter got caught in there," and she continued off into the woods for a badly needed bathroom break.

Her stream was interrupted by an impassioned shout from her seventeen year old son "Holy crow, Ma, come here quick!"

She ran to him as soon as possible without fully zipping herself up, all the while thinking 'This better be good.' And then she saw that his face was devoid of blood, he was so pale she feared he might faint, and there before her was a girl, just a child, battered, bloody, swollen and covered in what looked like bites from bugs and perhaps even animals. "Oh dear lord," was all she could say.

They reached into the back of the Woody and pulled out a blanket. They opened it up inside the wagon bed and gently lifted the girl from her resting place. Then they tried to give her water and at least rinsed her face. After a few minutes she managed to drink a few drops. Eventually they ended up pouring water onto a facecloth and arranging it so it would stay in her mouth. Just a little sucking would provide her with moisture. Then the son said, "I'll ask the

GPS for the nearest hospital." But his mother refused to let him do so. She wanted to take the girl home.

She said "Whoever hurt this child might be her next of kin; you read stories like that all the time so why would we put her back into the hands that may have beaten her. I'm a nurse, let's get her home and see what she needs. We can always take her to the hospital there, but she may need a little time away from this place." And what she was thinking, but did not say out loud was 'Anyway, you know your dad and I, God rest his soul, had always wished for a daughter, well maybe you just found your sister.'

And with that she closed up the Woody, repacked the table and chairs into the backseat, and tossed a sandwich to her son keeping one for herself. She would drive, think and eat her lunch; everyone knew that women were good at multi-tasking.

20

THE NIGHTMARE CONTINUES

wendolyn Perkins, Gwen to her friends, arrived back in Athol, Massachusetts with her son Mike, and the young girl. While her Woody had won no ribbons at the car show, she felt like a big prize winner to have found this poor abandoned child. She pulled her Woody into the garage; she and Mike were then able to carry the girl into the house and up to the guest bedroom. After they settled in a bit Gwen filled the bathtub and told Mike to carry the girl, fully clothed, to the tub where she would wash her and make an assessment as to the nature of her wounds. Gwen's plan was to undress her there and get Mike to help again when she had a towel about the child.

Once Katie was in the tub, Gwen sent Mike to the store with a list of supplies to both promote nutrition and to help her to bandage and mend the child. The list contained soups, Ensure, powdered milk, apple sauce, ice cream and multivitamins as keeping her hydrated and even resorting to hyper alimentation might be necessary. She knew that at first it would be like keeping a little featherless bird alive with constant feedings of very small amounts in near liquid form. Slowly she must be built back up in order to survive so much trauma and injury.

Then Gwen, although a bit overweight and out of shape, knelt at the side of the tub and gently began cutting away the filthy blood soaked clothing. Bleeding had stopped, but much of the girl's body was discolored and swollen. She certainly had at least one broken arm and it appeared that her head had sustained injuries. For awhile Gwen thought about the need to have the child's head examined to determine how much bleeding there might be on the brain. Then she dismissed the idea by thinking how resilient children were and that simply moving her to the hospital might add to her difficulties. They would give her some time and see in which direction she progressed.

When Gwen reached the girl's abdomen, to the tops of her thighs, she discovered extensive bruising and a tear in the vaginal area which had been bleeding. Gwen muttered "You don't have to be a Chief of Staff to know that this girl has been sexually abused!" and she tearfully and gently washed the child in this area. In hindsight she would realize that she had likely destroyed evidence, but at the time it seemed like the thing to do. Then she continued down the body grateful to find only one more suspicious area. The lower left leg too was swollen and bruised. Instead of waiting for the child to try and use it she decided it would be best to splint this too.

As Katie lay there, Gwen encouraged her to drink more water and tried to get her to speak. She did sip the liquid, but no coherent words emerged from her mouth. Then Gwen heard the car pull into the garage and knew that Mike must have returned with their supplies. She let the water drain from the tub and hurried to get more towels and a warm nightgown for their guest. There would be nothing but warmth, nutrition and pain relievers for this poor child for quite some time she vowed.

Gwen moved toward the garage doors into the house to see if she could help Mike carry things in so that they could care for the child immediately now that she had triaged the injuries. He suddenly burst into the house speaking loudly that she "was not going to believe what he found out!"

"And what might that be, Mike? And please don't shout with a sick person in the house!"

"Well," he said, "She is exactly what I am shouting about. I saw a newspaper at the grocery store and the headline was 'Girl from Eastern Connecticut Missing, Fear Foul Play'. Ma the whole area is looking for that kid; they even gave her name and printed a plea from her mother. She has a brother and a sister who are also broken-hearted but I guess the dad may be suspected of causing harm."

"Whatever her name is we shall never use it," replied his mother. "We do not wish to let anyone else consider that our guest is this missing child at least until she is able to say who she is herself AND wants to go back where all this happened. Right now, she needs rest and protection, and it is our duty to see that she gets it for as long as possible! Henceforth we shall call her 'Linda'. Linda wasn't the name in the paper was it? I had a friend with that name in school; we shall call her by that name."

Mike agreed to 'Linda' since the name in the paper was Katie, but he dared not mention this name out loud for fear of disturbing his mother further. "Good," she replied, "now let's go get Linda into bed."

After 'Linda' was warmed and placed in a flannel nightgown Gwen splinted her arm and leg. The child had a reaction when these areas were touched, but otherwise gave no real indication of being awake. Gwen slowly fed her Ensure and was warming the soup for later. She used her cell to call her personal physician's office and tell his nurse that she had another sinus infection. She begged them sweetly to just call in a script to the pharmacy as she didn't have time to let him look up her nostrils, but as a nurse she knew a sinus infection when she had one. As was their custom they agreed to phone it in and said she could probably pick it up by evening. "Good," she replied, "I wouldn't want my breathing to be compromised all night without the help, thank you."

Then she turned to Mike and asked him to swing by the pharmacy on his way home from the local pizza parlor saying that she simply did not have time to cook that evening. Gwen felt most pleased, she was making excellent clinical decisions and everything was falling into place. And best of all, she thought, I will soon have a sweet little daughter, and she will be safe from her evil father. Then she turned back to the girl and slowly encouraged her to take in more liquids.

Back in East Apple things were not going so well. Katie's mother and siblings were indeed frantic as were the neighbors next door who not only cared about Katie but worried about the stories that might spread about Grace and the terrible pain which Grace was experiencing at the loss of Katie. Also, there was some rather bizarre news that the State Police dogs had eventually led detectives to a shed on the gravel pit grounds of a neighboring town. The dog went crazy barking and leaping in the area and went on point at the shed.

But visual inspection revealed no sign of Katie. Then the officers went back with Luminol and sprayed much of the area, especially the shed, looking for blood evidence which is a reaction when Luminol meets blood. They found a terrific reaction in the shed meaning someone or something had bled considerably in that area. The problem was that they now had to compare Katie's DNA to the DNA found in the blood. This meant that Katie's DNA from her hair in a hairbrush at home had to be typed and compared to the type of blood in the shed. Everyone was holding their breath hoping that it would not be a match as so much blood had been lost; but also hoping it would be a match so that there would be some evidence, some lead as to Katie's location, because at this point the investigation had turned up nothing. It would take until the following morning to know.

The police were also a little suspicious of Mr. Jennings' behavior as he insisted on rushing right over to the scene of the bloody shed. Most parents would wait, maybe hold their other kids close, maybe even pray, but he wanted to see it with his own eyes. Of course the reason for this was because he could not believe that she was totally gone. He had expected that they would find some of her remains after the animals had finished with her, and he wasn't sure how she got into the shed itself.

But when he arrived on the scene one astute officer took note of the fact that Jennings' tire tracks matched at least one set of tracks left in that area. Was the murderer returning to the scene of the crime he wondered? Then he took photos and plaster casts of all tire prints.

21

KATIE-LINDA WAKES UP

After five days of continual feeding, cleaning, and talking to Linda, Gwen saw the child beginning to come around. Although a hospital would have been a better place for the badly injured girl, the dedication of her caretaker was truly admirable and was paying off as she appeared to be nearly out of her coma. The medications Gwen had scrounged up for her also kept the pain down as well as preventing an infection. Gwen hoped no one would ever question the prescriptions that she had forged for opioids or ask her too much about her sinus infections; she certainly wasn't selling drugs nor was she an addict, but her dear Linda required help with intense bone pain.

Now she gently asked the child what she remembered. Katie could recall nothing about how she was hurt; if someone else had been responsible for her injuries; or even who she was. She stated that when she was called 'Linda' it did not sound right, but she had no idea what name would sound correct. Her memory was jumbled and distant. Gwen was encouraged that if 'Linda' did not know who she was for long enough, it might be possible to get away with convincing her that she was really Mike's cousin and had been sent to live with them. She would do all she could to prevent the child from reading the newspapers for as long as possible. She didn't want the actual news stories to trigger Linda into remembering that she was Katie!

The plan now was to keep Linda inside the house until she could totally recover from her most serious injuries. If she went out with crutches it would naturally generate a lot of questions to which Linda didn't know the answers, and that Gwen wasn't yet sure how to answer. She was thinking of saying the child had been in a car accident that took her parents' lives and it was so traumatic that she had blocked it out. "Of course, you will understand that she cannot handle any questions," Gwen would add. But Gwen was a little fearful of telling this total lie in case the authorities should ever catch up with them. It would work better to say that Linda was found by the side of the road and begged them not to take her home for her father had done this to her, and she was very afraid. Then they might be able to say that they had no idea where she came from but only wanted to protect her. "Oh what to do," Gwen thought.

Back in East Apple, Katie's mother and siblings became more concerned and frantic for her safe return as each day passed. Her dad feigned similar feelings, but his concern revolved around his hope of escaping detection; so Katie remaining absent actually protected him. As for Grace, she paced the floors in her house wanting to somehow solve this problem; she believed she had let Katie down by not overcoming her dad when he had attacked Katie a few days earlier. Now Grace was certain that Mr. Jennings had killed her best friend and hidden her body.

Grace wondered if there was any part of her strange DNA that could assist her in finding out where Katie really was. She didn't think of snakes as having a wide range of contacts that might lead to locating a lost child. She also couldn't imagine that there were enough Giant Goliath Bird Eating Spiders to know what might be happening beyond their immediate group of underground tunnels, and she no longer thought that there was a possibility of Katie being close-by. What other special talent might she have with which to help Katie?

Then she thought of the portrait – did her biological father still have a way to view what was happening in a wide spectrum of the world? Could he know what was happening to Katie or if she was in the spirit world or still among the living? If he could tap into that information would he even tell Grace, or if he would tell Grace, would he expect a fee from her that was insurmountable? In the past he had always demanded a favor in return for his help, and that payment had often been difficult to make.

'If only the police could answer these questions' she moaned to herself. But maybe they could. Later that day, when Matt checked with the State Police Barracks he discovered some cause for optimism. It seemed that they were still working on their investigation of the crime scene. They knew that the blood found at the scene was that of Katie's, but they also found similar, but not identical DNA, indicating that Katie's father had also been at this shed. That DNA was taken before Mr. Jennings had made such a show of rushing over to the place where it appeared Katie had been injured. He could have masked the fingerprints which remained there, as he touched many things, but his DNA had already been found.

The other important piece of evidence was the tire tracks. Yes, Mr. Jennings' vehicle had left tracks within that entry to the gravel quarry, but they might not be able to sort older tracks out from the ones he had recently left. That is, a car similar to Jennings' was there probably as far back as the day of the kidnapping, but the police would have trouble proving it, as Jennings had been on the scene subsequently. When did he make which tracks, was a big question.

But there had been another set of tracks altogether different from Jennings'. And those tracks had stopped in the middle of the clearing and then turned and gone directly to the shed. When the officers had taken photographs and then plaster imprints of those tracks, the experts who reviewed their findings were rather amused. The imprints of the tires they discovered were from a specially made tire designed to be used on classic antique automobiles and would be whitewall tires created to show a car off. In fact, with a little research it was discovered that the particular tires which made the imprints from which they had a cast were called Firestone Classics, and were only sold in a few shops in New England.

Almost immediately the forensic experts were faxing copies of their prints to every dealer who carried them within a one hundred mile radius. There were three dealers who responded that they carried that particular brand and style: one in Rhode Island, one in Connecticut, and one in Massachusetts. The police also had the advantage of knowing from the imprints that these tires were new even though they were designed for a classic car. This made questioning the dealers a little more specific: how many such tires had they sold in the last few months? Only one dealer, the shop in Massachusetts, had recently sold a set.

The next question was "could the dealership determine to whom they had made their sale?" And they were able to answer this question because a sale as large as tires was paid for by a credit card, and the woman who had made the purchase often came to their shop as she kept an old Pontiac Woody in tip top condition, often competing with it in car shows. They provided the Connecticut State Police with the name: Gwendolyn Amesbury, her address and phone number.

Rather than calling Mrs. Amesbury and providing advanced warning to her, should she be a criminal element in this missing person's case, they decided first to make certain inquiries about her. The police in her location had no record of any calls to her house, and the Massachusetts' State Police claimed that she had no criminal record. Then the police searched for car shows on the day of the kidnapping as she was noted to be frequently involved with these events. There were none, but there had been one that ended the day before Katie was reported missing. It had taken place in Rhode Island and Gwendolyn Amesbury was a registered entrant. Then the police mapped out the most likely route Mrs. Amesbury would have traveled to return home from the Rhode Island show. It would have taken her prize Woody right by the entrance to that gravel quarry.

The State Police called Katie's mom and asked if she would like to go on a little ride with them. They did not know what they would find, but if this child had been traumatized they believed the best action that they could take would be to reunite mother and daughter as quickly as possible. It would also help establish their right to remove the child if her mother was with them; after all they would be dealing with the police from another State and were out of their jurisdiction.

They also knew they might need to protect Mrs. Jennings from some possibly horrible truth at the end of this journey, but they would face that if necessary.

So the little cavalcade from Connecticut headed to Athol and was to be met there by the Massachusetts' State Police.

22

YOU LOOK FAMILIAR

The Connecticut State Police waited by the side of the road about three houses down from the Amesbury home. It was here that they were met by the Massachusetts State Police whom they followed into the Amesbury driveway. An officer from each state approached the door while a local officer went around to the back of the house in case anyone should be attempting to make an unseen exit. The second Connecticut officer remained in the cruiser with Mrs. Jennings who was shaking with anxiety and the hope of seeing her daughter alive.

The second knock brought a high school age boy to the door. He said his mother was taking care of someone and would be right down then he yelled: "Mother, police!"

By the time Gwen arrived to greet the officers they were already well aware that she was tending to someone upstairs, so they simply said that they needed to see her patient. She took a step back, stuttered just a little and said, "Well first let me explain. We found this child in dreadful condition and it was obvious some male had assaulted her in all ways possible. I was so afraid that a member of her own family had done this to her that I decided to secret her away. And when we got her home, and I could see that I was capable of managing her condition, I am a nurse you know, that I just kept her here so that she would be safe."

The Massachusetts officer said, "Fine. We'll hear all about that later, but right now we would like to see the child." And Gwen walked them directly to the girl sensing that they were not going to put up with any delays.

The child seemed frightened by the unexpected intrusion after many days of only speaking to Gwen and Mike and feeling herself safely shutoff from the world. The policeman from Connecticut introduced himself to her and asked "Are you Katie Jennings from East Apple, Connecticut?"

"I'm not sure said the child. I think my name is Linda but Katie sounds familiar. My head was hurt and I'm just not certain."

The officer continued, "I wonder how you are doing? There is a lady with us waiting out in the car and she believes you are her daughter who disappeared from home during the night a couple weeks ago. Are you willing to have me bring her in and see if you recognize her? Because having seen several photographs of the missing child I would say that you are Katie. But you have certainly been banged up."

Katie's eyes were so wide open that she looked like a bug, all giant lenses, but she nodded in the affirmative that this lady could come and see her, even though her fear was palpable. Then the woman sounded as though she were running up the stairs and she went from the doorway to the bed as though traveling in a basketball game, no steps, just hurtled herself into Katie. And when Katie saw the woman flying toward her she was no longer frightened, she smiled for the first time since being beaten, "Mama," she said.

Now it was Gwen's turn to express happiness that these two had been reunited. She kept wringing her hands and saying "Thank God, Thank God. I am so happy for her that she has her own mother back and is not fearful of her."

But on another floor the police continued to question Mike who appeared to be an honest person and most cooperative. Maybe he didn't like playing in the background while his mother doted on this child; maybe he didn't like doing errands for this kid and housework so his mother could care for her; at any rate he told the police about everything he knew.

He explained that he and his mother had seen a news story about Katie when they first returned from the car show with her. She had also been on the front page of their local newspaper, not as the lead story, but as something important to be alert to, this missing girl, possibly in their area. But Mike explained his mother didn't think they should get mixed up in returning her until she was well enough to explain what had happened to her. If they sent her back into harm's way they would only be undoing all of their hard work and putting her at risk again. In another week or two they planned to start checking with the police back near where they had found the child.

The officer said, "In Connecticut?" and Mike said, "Yes."

The local police then had to bring both Amesburys in for questioning while the Connecticut police determined that Katie and her mother should return to Connecticut by ambulance. They certainly wanted Katie to be medically cleared before they questioned her further. It continued to be obvious that Katie was having some difficulty with her memory, but she was certain of who her mother was, although she also said nice things about Gwen Amesbury and wanted to hug her goodbye. The police reasoned that whatever Mrs.

Amesbury had done wrong she had not been the perpetrator of this abuse on the child.

Back on Cemetery Hill Road Grace paced the floors. She had seen the State Police vehicle take Mrs. Jennings away and her mind was hammering with different possible explanations for why this had occurred. Her most grim reckoning was that they must have found Katie, dead and Mrs. Jennings was to identify her body. Another thought was that they had found evidence of Mr. Jennings' wrongdoings and they wanted to show it to his wife before they arrested him so that she would be prepared. The reality of Katie having been found alive after two weeks of being missing never entered her head.

It was late in the day when she observed that Mrs. Jennings was brought home. Her behavior surprised the child spy. She was smiling, reached for the hands of each officer, and even gave a quick hug to the lieutenant. What can this mean thought Grace? Then with a stab of joy that was so sharp it was almost painful she blurted out loud, "She must be alive! Katie must be alive!"

And before Mrs. Jennings had reached her side door, Grace had run down two flights of stairs and was outside streaking through the grass toward her friend's mother. From her yard she yelled "Is Katie found? Is she alive?"

Mrs. Jennings, while seeming somewhat dazed, turned toward the girl and said, "Yes, dear, she is alive and doing quite well. I think she will be released by the hospital tomorrow." And then she slipped into her house to tell the details of this news to her family for they had heard it by phone but would be anxious to see their mother and to confirm it all.

Grace ran through the house finding her mother so that the words could be repeated, "She is alive and well!"

The next day, before Katie was sent home from the hospital, the police called Mr. Jennings. They stated, "That they were not pressing any charges at this time, but there appeared to be some anxiety in Katie whenever his name was mentioned and that they were not finished with their investigation. Would he be so gracious as to voluntarily leave home for two weeks so that they could tie up loose ends?"

Stammering and trying to give every sense of a man hurt by such a wrong track of concern, Jennings reluctantly agreed. To further demonstrate his injury, Jennings asked if the police could recommend suitable housing and a distance away for him. The officer replied, "Thus far that would be up to you unless you want to spend two weeks in a cell and reimburse the State for your meals? We are recommending this action, but we could get the judge to require it if you prefer." Jennings said nothing more on the matter. He was out of the house before Mrs. Jennings and the other children picked Katie up at the hospital.

Katie seemed truly happy to return. She went around the house touching things and smiling. She was remembering most everything. She did check to make certain that her dad was not home and she only seemed to fully relax when they confirmed that he was gone for awhile. Then she turned to her mother and said, "And is Grace the name of the girl next door?" When that was confirmed she replied. "I would like to see her as soon as possible."

23

ATTEMPTING ESCAPE

When Mrs. Jennings called Elena Maria the first thing she did was burst into tears. Elena Maria waited murmuring kind things until her neighbor was able to speak. Then she said, "Katie would very much like to see Grace. My husband is not at home; would you consider allowing Grace to come over? Elena Maria checked with Grace and turned back to the phone saying that Grace was most anxious to see Katie.

Within minutes the children were reunited and they too were in tears. They went into the Jennings's' playroom where they could be apart from the family who were clustered around the kitchen, television, and the computers in the living room. Mrs. Jennings listened to the two girls as they spoke, but only from a distance and just long enough to be certain that their tone was cordial. Grace had come a long way through this last transformation. Soon there were even giggles coming from the girls, age appropriate, but hard to believe given Katie's and Grace's recent ordeals.

Grace was invited to stay for supper and as soon as that meal was over the request was put in that Katie wanted her to sleep over in the very same bed with her. Katie added that it was the only way she would feel safe. Grace got on the phone with her mother who then had to speak with Mrs. Jennings, but it was soon decided that Grace was truly behaving "like a normal child" and Katie sincerely needed her to stay the night.

Grace wore one of her friend's nightgowns and they settled into bed for a long period of whispered stories. Grace thought about providing more details of her life but soon realized her friend might not be able to handle quite that much shocking detail so they stuck to the stories they held in common about the terrible way Mr. Jennings had treated them both. And several of the strangest things about Grace were already known by her friend.

"After your father stabbed me, and I was badly bleeding, he just wrapped me up and tossed me into some bushes in the yard to finish bleeding and to die. But, somehow, maybe because I had been dead before, I did not return to that state of death so quickly, and Scruffy found me in time," said Grace.

"But that is so similar to what he did to me," said Katie. "He abused me and then I could tell he wanted to kill me to shut me up. He didn't want my mother to know what a horrible, sick man he was. He would rather lose his child than have to deal with getting treatment and admitting the truth. He must need the females he touches to be helpless, totally helpless, in order to please himself." How sad to think that a child this young could comprehend the perversions of an adult male, her own father no less.

But, understanding him did not equal forgiveness. In fact, the more the girls talked the angrier they became. He had tried to murder them both. Facing that squarely only made them wish to do him grievous harm, even at the same level he had attempted on them, before there could be a third person so badly injured or dead. It seemed to them that the police now had two witnesses saying the same things about the same evil man. Were they too young to be credible? Was the life of an adult male worth more than the lives of two female children? They wanted to know what their value was in this crazy world or was Grace going to need to take the action that the authorities had not. They had to make a pact that if the police didn't do anything to Katie's father before he was supposed to return to their home, then Grace would step in. Grace just hoped that she would be able to count on her shape-shift to give her the strength and ability to do away with Mr. Jennings once and for all. If she remained in the body of this ten-year-old child she was uncertain as to how she would proceed.

Over the next few days the girls were nearly inseparable, both trying to sustain the happiness and strength of the other, as they steadied themselves to survive until the police took action. As they entered the second week of Mr. Jennings' restrictions from being home, the girls became more anxious since they knew of nothing being done to arrest him.

Mrs. Jennings understood how frightened Katie was of having her father return home. She asked her daughter if she should get a restraining order to keep him away. To her surprise Katie said, "I want the police to take action. If you have to do it then it won't be enough to hold him long. He needs to be punished; he needs to at least go to jail. Don't you get it, mother; he tried to kill me and Grace and left us both for dead! How are we supposed to live with a man who would murder us?"

Mrs. Jennings called the State Police Barracks and learned they finally had the necessary warrants and were headed out that afternoon to arrest him on two counts of attempted murder and two counts of sexual assault on a minor. He should be behind bars by night fall.

And so he was. The only problem for the girls and for society too, was that during his last days of freedom he had found a lonely and wealthy woman to befriend. He was also courting her hoping that she would love him enough to disregard what the newspapers were saying and to provide him with what he needed to make all this go away. What he needed first was money for bail, and then more money for the best possible legal representation. He promised her a golden ring on her finger just as soon as he could get divorced, and she allowed herself to believe him. She wasn't a stupid person, but she was needy, and he knew just where his words would be most effective. Before the police "came calling" for him he had a well known lawyer on retainer, and enough money in the bank to please any bondsman with his worth. He even used some of that money to give a flashy ring to his new girlfriend.

When the police took him away in handcuffs, he said the clichéd words "You'll never hold me, I'll be out of jail by nightfall." And he was only off by a few hours as bond wasn't set until the following morning and then his bail was paid and he was released. His girlfriend's chauffer picked him up from the detention center where he asked if he could swing by his wife's house for a few things. He was required to wait in the car a few feet from the house for she did now have a restraining order, but he enjoyed seeing her have to deal with "his servant" and thought perhaps this new relationship was going to work out.

Katie and Grace were at Grace's house when this was happening. They watched it all from a third story attic window so that they could see the car with Mr. Jennings in it, as well as the man coming to Katie's house to pick up his belongings. Katie was frantic. "Oh sure," she said, "He gets whatever he wants from our house and we won't even know where he is to keep an eye on him!"

Grace replied, "Don't frighten yourself, the police will have to know where he is at all times and your mother may require that information. We'll put it to good use. Wherever he is we'll just have to find a ride to that location and then I'll take care of him, I promise you that I'll get him. And this time he won't get the better of me, and I will finish the job if I have to do it with a spider web, or act like a boa constrictor, I'll end his miserable life."

Both girls smiled then, and decided to look through items stored in the attic to find any possible costumes in case they needed to be disguised for their journey. They were not afraid of eliminating him from the human race, as they already saw him as a miserable creature, but they would rather not have anyone know who had done this act or what that person looked like. The girls especially didn't want to look like two grade school-aged kids, as that might be a dead giveaway.

24

PREPARATIONS

Over the next few days the girls kept meeting at Grace's house to make decisions about which day they would travel to find Mr. Jennings and how they would travel. This also, of course, involved how they would appear because they did not want to be recognized as two girls. The police would instantly hear about a pair of kids visiting Jennings and know that Katie and Grace had sought their revenge. So they went through trunks Elena Maria had stashed in the attic as well as searching through racks set up in the attic storage closet.

Although Matt and Elena Maria had lived in this house for only a short period of time, they had accumulated many things. Perhaps much of it was left over from their pre-married days with costume party items, and some may have been left behind from previous owners, as a three story house with barns and outbuildings can be difficult to fully clean out. Whatever the explanation was the girls did find several items that would prove invaluable to their cause.

There was a shorthaired wig in light blonde which they powdered to make appear grey. There was boys' clothing as well as women's clothing in every conceivable style and size. There were shoes, boots and slippers, some needing to go to the dump, but others worthy of a little more use. And there were the kind of medical supplies left over from some relative's orthopedic injuries or long-ago decline. Such things as canes, crutches, braces, commodes, wheelchairs and back trusses were hung on rafters in far corners of the attic usually covered in plastic.

After careful analysis, and a lot of nervous giggling, they decided on their disguises. Grace would wear the powdered wig, clothing of an older lady complete with scarves, gloves and a shawl. She was considering wearing a leg brace just to keep the attention off her face which they would be struggling to make-up to appear wrinkled. Neither one of them had a clue as to how that could be done but they planned to Google 'wrinkle making' before the actual day arrived. She also planned to enter the building where Jennings should be, via a wheelchair; again to disguise her height as a child.

Katie could not wear stilts although they had actually entertained that idea. Therefore she would have to be a child, but changing her gender should be a significant help. So the plan was that Katie's hair would be pulled up under a masculine style cap and that she would be wearing a boys pants and a jacket. She would also wear slightly larger boots to make herself look more male and planned on chewing gum which would be bulging in one cheek.

With a boy helping his grandmother to get around, although they would obviously receive attention, they would not so easily be determined to be two ten-year-old girls. And if they fooled the cab driver they might simply be let out a few blocks from their ultimate destination so that the cabby could not say, with certainty what the location of their destination actually was or, who they were.

Each day they would discuss the total plan; how they would dress; how they would get to their destination; that Grace would enter the apartment of Mr. Jennings' alone; where Katie would meet up with Grace; and finally how they would return home. They even planned for the possibility that Katie might have to call the police if Grace was in Jennings' apartment too long. Neither one wanted that to occur but they had to have a back-up plan.

The night before they planned to punish Mr. Jennings the girls got their parents to agree that they could go off together for a picnic, but they promised to be home by early afternoon. It was strange to think that the parents of two molested little girls would let them wander on their own, especially with so many other bad things happening in the world, but it was almost as though their sense was that the worst had already happened so the kids would be okay. But they should not have taken these girls at their word.

The next morning they each packed a small lunch to make it appear that they were, indeed, going on a picnic. They also carried a bag which their folks presumed contained their picnic blanket and similar items; only it was filled with costumes. The wheelchair was impossible to disguise so they simply explained that all their stuff was kind of heavy and they could use the chair like a shopping cart to carry their provisions. Having covered all their bases they began their odyssey.

They had to walk several miles pushing the wheelchair containing their supplies. Being kids they sometimes took turns riding in the chair and passersby simply saw kids at play. Finally they were on the outskirts of the nearby city which cabs often used carrying students and workers. They went behind a garage on the property of a house which looked abandoned. All the curtains were drawn, there was mail piled up outside a mailbox, and trash cans stood empty and uncovered by the side of the road. There was also a skim of pollen on the surface of the driveway which indicated no sign of any use.

The girls went around behind the garage and were pleased to see that the view back there was obstructed from the neighboring houses. It took them only a few minutes to change into their disguises; it would have been even less time if they had not also been laughing at each other. Then they straightened up and Grace said, "This is serious, deadly serious!"

Grace got into the wheelchair and Katie acted the part of the dutiful grandson helping his Grammy along the sidewalk as they hunted for a cab. Eventually a cab pulled up and Katie, who had practiced the voice for days, gave the driver the address of the apartment in which his lady friend had put him up. The driver said, "You know you have to pay for this ride, right sonny?"

And Katie answered, "Don't worry dude, we've got money." And off they went to a part of the area in which they had little familiarity. It was close to the wealthy district which must be where his "girlfriend" lived, but it was on the edge. They both rightfully assumed that this must be where the wealthy housed their top help when not living with them.

The girls had studied Google Earth and had chosen an address which they knew to be about three blocks from Jennings apartment. They were let out of the cab at that address, paid the fare, and the cabby helped "the old lady" get settled into her chair. Then they watched the cab driver pull away before they took off in the direction of their true destination.

By now they were both fairly nervous. It might not seem strange for an elderly lady to have a slight tremor but the young boy who was accompanying her was also pretty shaky. They hoped that no one was observing them too intently or for too long. Then they were at the front stoop of the apartment building which they sought. It was more of a multi-family dwelling than an actual high rise apartment structure. This building might well have been a single family unit when it was new, and then it was converted into apartments as the neighborhood aged and the price of oil rose.

A ramp had been constructed along one side of the building to permit handicap access in compliance with the laws, no doubt. They entered that way in order to maintain their disguises a little longer. Here, in the interior corridor, they would set up their command station with Katie waiting in the hall and holding onto her sister's cell phone which she had confiscated the night before. Her plan was to help her sister find the phone that night when they were finished with it.

Now Grace pulled off the 'elderly garb' and once again appeared as a kid. Then she asked Katie to turn away while she used every ounce of her concentration to become her copperhead self. They had been thinking about it for so long, and with such intensity that it worked. Katie turned back and saw a large cobra with its head raised.

For a moment Katie didn't know what to do until the cobra slithered into the chair and waited for Katie to wheel it to Jennings' door where Katie would knock and then run.

25

SNAKE CHARMER

G race had not had an easy time making the transition to snake which had just taken place. She had concentrated on the change so hard that her head hurt. In fact, most of her bones were in pain from their rapid collapse. And Katie might not have noticed how her body burst through the clothing she had been wearing, but she would have a difficult time finding something suitable to wear home later. Still, Grace could only think about her mission. The last time she had confronted this evil man had almost cost her life.

Then, while waiting for the door to be answered, it finally struck her; she had transformed into a cobra not a copperhead! How could this happen when it was copperhead DNA that coursed through her veins? But that was what she had become, a hissing, coiling, poisonous cobra. Her thoughts during the metamorphosis were 'make me strong, powerful, deadly; I want to show him he cannot treat little girls with total disregard. He may hurt us and even kill us, but in the end some of us will rise up stronger and smarter and more lethal than he. I want to triumph today!' And with that determined spirit and mantra for strength, Grace had by-passed the copperhead strength and become a devastating cobra!

The apartment door was suddenly yanked open and Mr. Jennings stood looking out over the balcony that formed a corridor leading by the apartment doors. They were on the second floor as the ramp had wound along the building and climbed to this height. As he briefly looked forward the snake slithered inside the apartment leaving the wheelchair vacant.

Jennings, finally noticing the chair, kicked it over against the railing cursing "some idiot" for playing a practical joke. He then reentered his apartment with a slam of the door behind him. The cobra was waiting under his couch. Grace had decided to see what he was doing on this, his final day of life. He simply continued to mutter and went back into the bathroom where he had been preparing to shave. His mood became more upbeat, and it was apparent he was preparing to see his "honey".

Good, thought the cobra, when he is late for their meeting let her come over here and discover his body once I am finished with it! Then she decided to strike without further ado as Katie was anxiously waiting below. The bathroom was small and cheaply constructed with a painted plywood cabinet over the sink and large gaudy light bulbs gleaming into his face as he shaved.

Grace decided to let him die with a little thrill to think about in hell. As he twisted his sinister mouth to one side so he could better shave the opposite area, she reared up to almost her full length. This placed her cobra face right behind his ear in the mirror. The sides of her face that resemble gills were fully flared out and, with her large eyes and twitching tongue, gave just the right effect to put a death scream in his throat and to render him nearly comatose.

The mirror also helped to make this production eerier as Jennings didn't know which way to turn; in his terror, which was his right and which his left; just where was that snake? He turned the wrong way and she bit his neck. Unfortunately, she missed the jugular and he had now regained a little bit of his lost mind. He swung at her eye with his razor nicking her flesh but narrowly missing the orb. Then the fight was on. He tried repeatedly to either get away or to swing back with his blade. If he had just done one or the other, he might have been alright, but attempting to perform two, somewhat opposed tasks, sealed his fate, cast him to doomsday, led to his annihilation.

The fight was on, a tall overweight man in his undershorts with a razor blade inside of his manual shaver vs. a long sleek cobra breathing venom and revenge as she slithered, leaped and coiled about him. He struck her several times with his weapon drawing a sort of blood, but not a great quantity. And each time his blade or arm connected with her slick skin she would raise her head above him and hiss in a manner that made him scream. Those were the times when he attempted to reach the door, but her coil would trip him up, and he would fall harder and faster each consecutive time she pulled him down.

He decided to try and carve away at whatever piece of her was available to his hands, and he grabbed near the end of her tail trying to hold fast while he wacked blindly with his blade. This did not please Grace. She moved her head up the loose leg of his undershorts. She saw a hairy looking sack that was hanging between his legs and which she knew held some responsibility for the ways he treated women and girls. She bared her fangs, watched as her venom began to lubricate them, and then sunk those puncturing machines deeply into his scrotum.

This is not pretty to report, and it pains the writer to have to describe this, but we all know a man who would drug adult women and make them miserable to gain pleasure for himself; and a man who would actually attempt to murder his own daughter and a little neighborhood girl for his own benefit and gratification, cannot survive a story such as this when the spirit has the power to do otherwise. Mr. Jennings must die, and the child who is half spirit will be the one to eliminate him.

The cobra bite caused Mr. Jennings to scream both in agony and in terror. This sensitive part of him reacted to the assault, and his bloodstream quickly sent the message that he was in trouble. His brain visualized what the feeling in his pants must mean and he was nearly dead from fear before the venom had traveled very far. Then he had a seizure followed by a second one in which he flopped about the floor unable to control his muscle spasms, foaming at the mouth, trying to sit up and then collapsing again and losing control of his bowels. And then he was dead. Out on the floor and chilling; he never would finish that shave or meet his girlfriend for lunch; or molest anyone else ever again.

The next steps were up to Grace. She looked at her cobra body and thought "Okay body, let's do this." And she blinked and concentrated and strained, but nothing happened. Then she reviewed her wounds and told herself that they were hardly cause for alarm, she would be fine. But still nothing happened. Finally, she looked at Mr. Jennings laying there and thought of all the horrible things he could do no more. The cobra smiled and then it began its transition back to Grace. It seem slower than she had expected. When it got just below her waist it stopped. She was a girl with a snake tail, sort of a desert mermaid.

She grabbed Jennings shirt off a chair to cover her top half and then slithered out the apartment door without another look behind her. She easily reached the wheelchair undetected by neighbors, used her arms to reach the seat, and then tossed her shawl over the lower part of her body almost fully covering her tail. Now she turned those wheels so that she was soon heading down the ramp and into Katie's arms where they hugged for a full minute. Then Grace said, "it is over, he won't be back this time." And they loaded up the chair and headed for home deciding they would make it on their own efforts without a cab.

After about a mile Katie suggested that Grace might want to walk for a bit since they were now far from the apartment and that pushing Grace was feeling heavy. Grace suggested that they pullover behind a tree that they were approaching. When they did, Grace slowly raised the shawl so that Katie could see the snake's tail. Katie then used some words that shocked Grace as she did not know her little friend had such a vocabulary.

"What are we going to do?" asked Katie.

Grace said, "I have no idea, but I may have to find out if my parents really love me."

26

SHE LOVES ME YES,
SHE LOVES ME NOT

Grace asked Katie to bring her to the bulkhead of her cellar. Then Katie had to carefully ease the wheelchair down six old cement stairs. From here Grace explained that the only hope for her was if Katie could get her upstairs and into her own bed without anyone seeing her tail. She needed more time to figure out how to approach her mother, how to explain this transformation. A few hours of "sick-time" in bed might allow her mind to function well enough to figure out a solution.

"So how do I get you upstairs to bed," asked Katie?

Then Grace told Katie about the secret trapdoor leading into her parents' closet from the basement. The biggest hurdle was that Grace would have to climb the steps that fall to the cellar from that trapdoor. Just how was she to manage that?

Grace's arms are strong. She asked Katie to walk behind her going up those steps so they will have the strength of one and a half people to get two up to her parents' room. They decide to try it before they can talk themselves out of it, for there are scary elements such as potentially falling off these steps. Katie finds the rope hanging against a wall in the cellar and gives it a yank; the stairs slowly float down to them. Once they struggle up, with a few close calls, they are in Elena Maria's bedroom closet.

Katie peeks from the closet into the bedroom and confirms that it is empty. Grace then wiggles like "the snake she is" out of the closet, through the bedroom, down the hall, and into her own room. It takes a bit of a shove from Katie to get Grace onto the bed as her tail is heavy, but soon she is in bed and wearing the top half of her nightgown.

Katie will now go home. The plan is that she will find Elena Maria and say that she has just tucked Grace into bed as Grace started to have a bad headache toward the end of their picnic. She hastily adds, "We looked for you, but then decided you must be busy with baby Mattie so we just went on up. That was okay, wasn't it?"

Elena Maria stammers a bit, "Well, of course, you are welcome here, anytime, or any place. I will go right up to her. I just don't know how I missed you kids, and I feel badly that Grace isn't feeling well."

"That sounds good, Mrs. Nelson. I'll head home now, but please let me know how Grace is doing. Nice to see you," Katie adds and then makes her exit.

As the baby is asleep, Elena Maria rushes up the stairs. She walks softly toward Grace's room and pokes her head in the door. "Hi, sweetheart, she says. May I come in?" And seeing Grace's nod she walks forward asking, "How are you feeling?"

When she heard her mother coming toward her down the hallway Grace had an immediate rush of adrenaline. She could feel her heart racing, her breathing becoming more rapid, and tension along her brow. She was totally stricken with fear regarding having to reveal her tail to her mother. Tears were even forming in her eyes. Then she felt a sort of whooshing under the sheets with a dull ache in her abdomen. Suspiciously, she pulls the sheets away from her body far enough so that she can look down upon herself and there she finds her two human legs and a spot of bright red blood between them. "Mother," she practically shouts, "I think I have started my first period!"

Elena Maria is a bit taken aback for a moment, and then she responds as any good mother should with an, "Oh, honey, that is wonderful. You should feel better very soon. Ten is a little on the young side but you are almost eleven..." and she is interrupted before she is able to finish.

"Almost eleven or one hundred and thirty, depending on how you do the counting."

"Well, yes," replies Elena Maria. "The very good news is that this means you are human, not so much a spirit, because you are aging and maturing like the rest of us!"

Grace sat there wondering if a person, who could shift into a snake, could be labeled as human, and decided that apparently she could be. This was not the time to tell her mom about becoming a cobra, not at all.

While Elena Maria was finding the sanitary supplies for Grace, and considering just how to give her recommendations for use and comfort, the Jennings next door were about to face a far more complicated life change. The police were once again at their door and this time the news was grim. Out in the yard they told Mrs. Jennings that her husband had died while in an apparent altercation with an unknown person who must have broken into his apartment.

His place was torn up with broken furniture and papers strewn everywhere and several wounds were inflicted on his body. The medical examiner would eventually perform an autopsy and supply them with the exact cause of death, but those results could take a few days. In the meantime did Mrs. Jennings suspect any particular individual of committing this crime, and could she account for her whereabouts throughout the earlier part of the day?

She seemed both shocked by the news and bewildered. "I was expecting that we would be seeing him in court in the next few weeks, but I had no idea someone would want him dead. The children will be shocked too, although I must tell you that he had a girlfriend who bailed him out of jail recently. Perhaps she knows something about this," said Mrs. Jennings. "Also, I'm fairly certain he had made a lot of enemies at work, mostly women colleagues. Maybe one of them was sick of reading about him in the papers and decided to put an end to him. I have no idea."

"Well, if you think of anything," said the officer, "please let us know. And we are all happy that your little girl was found and recovered from her injuries. If she is around I'd just like to see her for a few minutes, maybe even give her the news about her father with you present, of course."

Mrs. Jennings felt she had to agree to this so the next thing they did was to bring Katie outside to join them. Katie drew her breathe in deeply when told her dad was dead, but did not seem particularly shocked or at all sad. The officer even said, "You don't seem too broken up about your dad?"

And the little girl replied, "My daddy did terrible things to me and to Grace. He would have been happy if I had died and he never had to see me again, so I'm probably better off without someone who hates me, but maybe later I'll feel sad."

The officer simply tipped his cap and said that he could understand that. And then he and Mrs. Jennings went inside to tell the other two children.

Later, as the officer was about to leave their home, he seemed to have an afterthought. "Tell me," he asked Katie, "your little friend Grace lives right here next door to you, correct? She didn't like your father very well at all did she? I mean she claimed to have been very badly hurt by him and was waiting for us to arrest him, right?"

"That's right," said Katie, looking at the officer as though to say, so what else is new, he molested us both. But she held her tongue and just held his gaze.

"Well," he said, perhaps just a little intimidated by this bold ten-year-old child, "I was thinking that since I am here already I should check in with that family, tell them the tragic news, and find out where their Grace girl was today."

27

PATHOLOGY

The police officers knocked on Elena Maria's door right after they left the Jennings' house. They noted that Mrs. Nelson was friendly and seemed genuinely shocked and disturbed to hear that Mr. Jennings had apparently been murdered. But she did not respond well when they asked if they could speak with Grace. They explained that they just wanted to be able to respond to any questions she might have, but her mother said she could handle any questions from Grace herself.

Then they said that they also wanted to clarify Grace's whereabouts that day, just to rule out any questions that could come up in the future since, not long before, she had a rough time with Mr. Jennings. That was when Mrs. Nelson visibly bristled. She said her daughter had spent the day on a picnic with Katie Jennings and was now home in bed as she was a bit under the weather. Her body language was clearly a road block; they weren't going any further in that house! So, since it was a low priority to question the girl, and since she was a

132

minor, and her mother was refusing them, they respectfully backed off and headed to the station.

The two houses on Cemetery Hill Road were shaken by the death of Mr. Jennings. His children and wife suffered from conflicting feelings as there was still some love alive for him, but it was rather diminished from what might have been expected within a family. And the Nelsons' felt the jolt anyone feels when learning that someone they know has passed away, especially if that passing is untimely; but they also felt a sense of relief given this man's cruelty to women and especially to their daughter. Also, somewhere in Elena Maria's heart was a nagging concern about the officers' interest in Grace. That seemed to undermine her sense of security and peace of mind.

The following day the state pathologist began the forensic workup on this new murder victim. She was an older and very experienced doctor considered to be on the top of her field. She had anticipated finding a stab wound or bullet entry sites, signs of hemorrhaging in the eyes, or even marks on the neck, but there was nothing like that. What she did observe was that this man died of multiple organ failures; everything gave up on him within a short period of time. Given that he was relatively young and healthy up until the day of his death, he must have been poisoned. She drew blood, took tissue and hair samples, and had them sent to Toxicology; then she examined the contents of Mr. Jennings' stomach to see what he had ingested and when.

The stomach contents were rather mundane. No clues were offered by the toast, banana and cereal he had eaten. Even his multiple vitamins proved to be a benign addition to the morning meal. Perhaps someone had stuck a needle in him, was her next thought. She began to reexamine his body especially in areas where other victims had been attacked by those attempting to administer sinister drugs.

Nothing, and then she suddenly felt foolish for she had overlooked his gonads assuming that their swollen condition was a side effect of all the factors that had gone wrong with him. But maybe he had been attacked in that very protected and hidden area of the male body.

She began to examine his testicles. They appeared to have been swollen at the time of death, and might have been red, although their coloring would have changed post-mortem. She speculated on the coloring simply because an injury in that area would have led to a rise of that color on the surface. After a few minutes using an electronic magnifying glass she did detect two distinct puncture wounds, that appeared more indicative of a bite mark than of an attack with a hypodermic needle. Yes, pending the findings of the toxicology report, Sally was almost certain that the deceased had been bitten in the testicles and that this bite was so powerful as to lead to his multiple organ failure.

Before the toxicology report was even completed, Dr. Sally, for that was what everyone called her, went a step further and began investigating what animal, biting with two teeth, could produce enough poison to cause death so quickly in a grown man of otherwise good health. It did not take long for her to narrow the search down to one particular category of snakes; the Elapidae. Among the most prominent members of the Elapidae were the mamba and the cobra. Now poisonous snakes are found on almost every continent, but this family was most likely to be found on the continent of Africa and in jungles.

One problem with the wound and the effects on the body was that it is very difficult to detect precisely which snake had done this damage. The family of snakes could be identified because their group does such lethal damage, but it would be impossible to know for which snake authorities might need to be looking. Of course such snakes in the wilds of Connecticut would be unexpected but just as lethal.

Dr. Sally decided to report that her findings would remain inconclusive until she received the toxicology findings. There was no sense in her sticking her neck out, with what appeared to be a farfetched conclusion, when the laboratory might make a precise and more reliable determination. Still, she was very curious and would have to state to the team that puncture wounds had been made into the scrotum.

While Dr. Sally was writing up her findings to date, her mind was also working at another problem. Hadn't she been in a hospital meeting fairly recently when something else out of the ordinary had come up about Elapidae? Wasn't that little girl who had appeared to "come back from the dead" found to have weird DNA? Didn't her DNA contain a mixture of arachnid and cobra genes? Was she remembering this correctly?

Then she shook her head and dismissed the thought, surely they would be locking her up if she put forth such a theory. Certainly, no ten-year-old girl had bitten this man to death in his private parts. And her blood contained the DNA; this didn't mean that she, or any part of her, could produce venom.

Dr. Sally remained disquieted, restless; finally she said out loud "Oh, what the heck, I might as well just look up that girl's name in case she lives next door to this Jennings guy or some other such weird coincidence." And so she did see the name Grace Nelson, and chuckled for a moment that Grace lived on Cemetery Hill Road, until she grasped the fact that although Jennings had died in an apartment on the edge of town, his legal address was also on Cemetery Hill Road. "Holy microbes," she muttered. "There does seem to be a snake in the grass on that street! Maybe I'd better prepare the boys for a bit of a surprise."

When she met with the detective in charge of this murder case he listened intently and respectfully. But lights were flashing in his mind that this old girl had looked at one corpse too many and was now seeing boogie men and little green snakes in her computer. He said, "Well, Dr. Sally, I do thank you for preparing me for any eventuality. Lord knows what could be next, but I think you and I should keep this snake theory to ourselves at least until the report comes back from the lab, as you say. Then we can start combing the hay out there on Cemetery Hill. It would be a mighty strange way for a little girl to kill a 'fella' although he was suspected of doing terrible things to that child. We'll just have to wait a couple days."

When Dr. Sally left, he just shook his head and said to his assistant, "All that education doesn't mean you can't slip under the Petri dish a little with stress and a few years on you."

The assistant had originally read those same reports that Dr. Sally had just pulled up. Her thoughts were that there could well be some truth hidden in there. She also thought that she couldn't think of a better way to get revenge on a molester than to take him out at the source of his misery. If he was forcing himself on women and girls maybe someone had thought of a way to eliminate his problem whether he lived or he died. There was something about Machiavelli that she had always liked.

28

A PERIOD OF GRACE

Grace felt much calmer now that Mr. Jennings was removed from her life as well as from Katie's. Knowing that he was right next door or could return at any point in the night to hurt one of them had always kept her from being at peace. And the more she thought about his attempting to kill them both the prouder she was of her actions which took his life. Still, her therapist would not approve nor would her deeds be in harmony with her medications, but when an act really needed to be performed, she could apparently move beyond the calm of the medications. The way she viewed it, the medications influenced her to act as would a reasonable person; when a reasonable person had to defend herself or be killed, then it was okay for her to act out even with aggression.

She wondered further if her initial troubles in transforming her shape, as when she ended up an arachnid although she strongly visualized the snake, were due to the influence of the drugs she took. She vowed to forgo those medications if she could ever predict another time in which she must convert to a snake. All the time she was thinking this, however, she prayed that such a metamorphosis would not be required of her. At this point Katie was the only person on earth who knew of her ability to shift form, and Grace was much safer if it remained this way.

She and Katie had a scheduled picnic in her backyard that Elena Maria was catering for them. It would be good to be alone with Katie long enough to discern what thoughts and feelings might be troubling her friend; after all it was her dad that they had terminated. But when they got together Katie simply shrugged her shoulders at the mention of her father. She said, "I wanted to cry over him, you know, really feel blue that I would never see him again, but he had beat it out of me. I didn't have any sentimental feelings left in me for him. I tried to conjure them up but the pain and anger for how he had treated me and you, and many people really blocked the happy memories if there really were any. It was like those positive thoughts and feelings had been choked back into a crevice in my mind that had slammed shut and been sealed off by a glacier. They are gone."

Grace thought about her friend's words and phrases before she responded. "I guess you will be okay as long as the environment doesn't get so hot that your glacier melts and you start to regret our actions," said Grace.

Then they returned to the lunch. They had homemade sweet and sour pickles which Elena Maria had made with Grace, egg salad sandwiches with the crusts cut off, tuna sandwiches, potato chips, and very fudgy brownies. This was accompanied by pink lemonade which tasted a bit strange when consumed next to the pickles, but for two farm girls eating on a folding table next to the barn on a sunny day, it was just about perfect. They even got to the point of giggling and revealing more confidences. Grace told Katie that she had started her periods and Katie thought that was early because her big sister had just begun. "My mother says I am old for my age", was all Grace added.

Scruffy forced his way into the picnic. He had done a tour of the property and marked the property boundaries as only a male dog will do, but human contact was almost his favorite experience of each day. Naturally, the number one joy in Scruffy's life was eating and the trigger that kept bringing him back to the girls was that they had opened the basket that had been sitting near their feet. Some things within the basket had sent a scented message to him, but when the lid was off the container, and the girls had removed the aluminum foil, he felt the tuna smell calling his name as with a megaphone. If humans did not wish to share their meals why would they keep putting such delectable concoctions into their mouths? Couldn't they stick to cottage cheese or tea; these foods would not be torturing a poor dog.

The girls were happy to see the dog come running toward them. He had been their hero more than once so in a way this celebration was for Scruffy too. He had notified the family when Grace had been left for dead and needed emergency attention. Maybe this once, thought Grace, no one will mind if we feed him from the table. Besides we are outside.

So bits of sandwiches and chips traveled underneath the table in small amounts where they were gleefully consumed by the dog. The girls did caution each other not to feed him too many chips as they were pretty certain that wasn't a good food for dogs. They also had both heard that chocolate was poison for dogs and thus they were noble, making certain to eat the brownies themselves, not even leaving crumbs for the dog. Scruffy never knew what he was missing as the tuna's tantalizing smell had full command of his brain.

Eventually, the girls picked up their picnic repacking it into the pretty lidded basket in which it had been served to them and took it into the kitchen in Grace's house. They recycled the paper products and cleaned the foil to be dried and used many more times. It was then, with Elena Maria upstairs with Mattie, that Katie asked what Grace had done with their disguises from the previous week. Grace said she had been alone in the house the day before when her mother and brother had gone for a stroller walk. She had used this opportunity to replace things exactly as they had been stored prior to the girls' using them.

Grace said, "I wanted to burn everything, but I was afraid for two reasons. First, somebody might notice any smoke the fire would make, and secondly, what if one of my folks wanted to use something like the wig again for a party? Or, what if they wished to loan the wheelchair to a friend or one of us had a temporary need for it? How would I explain the disappearance of so many things? I think they would immediately think I was up to my old tricks again."

"But," Katie said, "I may have spilled a little dressing onto those boys' trousers I was wearing. Will anyone notice?"

Grace replied, "I'm sure no one will ever even ask about any of it. I was just trying to be cautious and cover our tracks. The dressing will evaporate or something in no time. We are safe; we don't fit their idea of who might have murdered your dad." And Katie nodded in the affirmative because she too felt that they had been too clever to be found out.

Besides, they both agreed, they were two little girls who had been beaten and savaged by this man, how would anyone imagine that they could get the better of him? What power did they have, just helpless little girls who were terrified of this man?

Unfortunately, they both knew that they would be attending Mr. Jennings funeral the next day. The saving grace was that it would be quick and at the gravesite so that there would be no long speeches.

No one really wished to eulogize Mr. Jennings, not co-worker or kin. The minister said he would find a few fitting words and leave it at that. The church had not been interested in holding an indoor service for him and besides there was still COVID to be considered. They would sing a hymn and drop flowers into the burial site then Katie visualized that they would walk away and never come back. And that is pretty much what took place at the funeral for Jennings.

However, the day after this brief service the police detectives called Matt at the University. They wanted to meet with him, separate from the family, as soon as possible. There were some unusual findings during the autopsy and as a scientist they simply wanted his read on the possible explanations. Matt quickly added that his knowledge of physiology, as a psychologist, was primarily focused on the brain. They hastily replied that they felt certain he was the man for these questions. That was when Matt knew that this little questioning must have something to do with Grace.

29

MORE QUESTIONS

At the insistence of the police Matt agreed to drive over to the barracks for a discussion of their "unusual findings." Due to the COVID pandemic, even though it appeared to be tapering off, the University was not yet open to the public, thus he would go to them. He did want to avoid the police presence in his own home knowing how it might frighten Grace as she had already been through so much.

He arrived and was treated cordially and respectfully, some even called him Dr. Nelson. He wondered if he was being 'set-up for the slaughter'; that is, did they have very difficult questions they were intending to ask and did not want him immediately alert or on the defensive. He would be aware and just breathe normally as he really did have nothing to hide nor did his sweet Grace. After all the turmoil in which Grace had been the center: deaths, near deaths and much threatening talk, as well as her actual attack by Jennings, he felt almost jubilant that she was so innocent in this situation. He sat back and thought "Bring it on boys!"

There was coffee and small talk. The officers had the good graces to even ask about his family and research, but all these polite delays were minutes during which Matt could feel them building up to something. Then they asked again about Grace's whereabouts on the day Jennings was killed. He repeated what he and Elena Maria had said from the beginning; Grace had gone on a walk and a picnic with Katie for much of the afternoon, and then they had come back to the house where Grace went immediately to bed with a stomach ache.

The police were curious about what might have made his daughter feel sick that day. Matt loved this part, he played dumb. "What do you mean, officer, what made her feel sick?"

"You know," said the policeman, "Why was a healthy ten-year-old girl in bed so early in the day. Had something upset her perhaps?"

"I know of nothing that had upset her by that point. When Grace had gone to bed none of us were aware that Katie's father had passed away. It was somewhat later that we heard the news."

"Then I repeat," said the officer almost gleefully, "What do you suppose put this child in bed so early in the day? What made her sick?"

"Oh, that" said Matt, "My wife tells me that Grace had her first menstrual period and like many girls didn't feel so well this first time. Do you need proof of that? I hardly consider this police business." It was Matt's turn to feel gleeful, and the red on the officers' faces was very rewarding. "Was there anything else you wanted to ask me?"

After stammering a few minutes the more senior officer said that they wanted Matt to be aware of something odd uncovered in the autopsy. There was blood on the decedent's shirt, and some of that blood had not been his. In fact some of it was not from a human.

"Well, what are you talking about here," asked Matt?

The officer said the blood of a particular group of snakes had been identified. Not only that, but as things looked at this point, the lethal weapon, or the cause of death, was likely to be that same snake. The body had contained two bite marks or small puncture wounds placed into the scrotum of Mr. Jennings and causing a complete organ failure via its lethal venom. Mr. Jennings had been killed by a snake!

Matt said he found that most shocking, but what did that have to do with Grace? And then he remembered the workup of her DNA after she had been found unexpectedly alive. And he looked at the officers with widened eyes and a voice registering shockwaves as though it was part of the Richter scale during a volcanic eruption. He blurted out: "Surely you don't think that a ten-year-old girl who was snake bitten and therefore had some alteration reflected in her DNA could become an actual poisonous reptile, do you?" And his voice was raised several decibels.

He continued: "You said that you wanted me here as a scientist that my professional background might be of some help to you? Well, I shall give you my professional opinion as a psychologist, and as a father and a human being. No fucking way, you guys, that my beautiful young daughter is a murderous snake. No fucking way! Am I clear?"

"Dr. Nelson," the younger officer started, "We can see when you say it all out loud that it doesn't quite make sense. We didn't mean to shake your podium, just wanted to rule out this possibility. Certainly Grace has a unique history, and frankly we didn't know what to think. No offense intended."

But Matt was mightily offended and also a bit embarrassed that he had lost his cool. He wanted nothing more than to get out of there before he took a swing at one of the cops. So, rather abruptly, the meeting disbanded by mutual consent as none of them wanted to go any further with this line of inquiry, at least at this time.

Matt drove back to the University, but he did not go into his office even though that meant leaving his briefcase overnight, after all he was mostly paperless anyway with computers in two locations plus a laptop. Instead he drove to the University's dairy bar. The University of Connecticut's Dairy Bar had been famous for generations and with good reason. The grass fed cows gave their milk and cream to a business that made excellent ice cream in many flavors and used fresh ingredients. On a sunny day folks drove from hours away just to have a cone and look out on the bucolic pastoral life of the agricultural portion of the school. Matt wasn't going for the view or the notion of calming down in this setting. He wanted to bring some wonderful ice cream home as a treat for his wonderful family. He saw a half gallon of chocolate almond, one of strawberry ice cream, and a new flavor called 'Husky Tracks' as a way for a father to say 'I love you'. He didn't want poor little Grace to ever have to doubt that again.

Once he procured the ice cream it was a very short ride home to Cemetery Hill Road where he knew they had ample freezer space, and it would be a lovely evening. He muttered under his breath that he had never known a snake that liked ice cream, but he knew he was still angered by what had transpired at the police barracks and would have to drop that before he got home. He should have called ahead to see if Elena Maria wanted him to grill tonight, that would fit in nicely with the ice cream theme. Still, he was early, and there was time to run to the store for burgers and dogs if Grace and Elena Maria were in the mood. That would be a pleasure.

When he got home there were no stories of molesting neighbors, or any workmen mysteriously poisoned, or portraits on the wall that could reach into the past and perform magic, everything seemed peaceful. Scruffy came to greet him and probably would have been happy to carry the ice cream.

While their very pleasant evening was getting underway Grace asked if Katie could stay for dinner and both parents assured her that would be fine as long as it was okay with her mother. Katie ran next door and came back happy to say it was okay for her to stay.

Then Matt made patties and started the grill, and Elena Maria had the girls shuck some corn. Although it was store bought this time of year, grilling caramelized the kernels and gave the corn a very freshly picked flavor. The table was being set on the porch for the first time that season, and all seemed in a good mood.

But across town, and two miles up the highway, the police officers in the barracks where Matt had just been questioned were asking themselves a few questions. What do we have to go on? Do we need a herpetologist? Let's comb that apartment complex and that neighborhood where Jennings died to see if anyone is missing a pet snake or used to work in the circus? Also, neighbors reported seeing someone being pushed in a wheelchair by a boy, someone they had never seen before. Let's see if we can get more on him or her and check to see if any cab companies or Uber drivers dropped off or picked up an odd couple like that on the twenty-fourth.

30

POLICE DETECTIVES

The State Police allocated three detectives to this case. Yes, it appeared to be a homicide; but the victim had been a lowlife character who may very well have been 'taken-out' by one of his own kind, someone from the underbelly of life. Not a high priority like a missing child had been. There was no one for whom there was a great outcry of sympathy and compassion. Still, if the general public found out he had died as the result of a snake bite in his scrotum it might have generated some interest at least in the tabloids. No one would be publishing a photograph of this, which was certain.

Then they were reminded that Jennings had some political connections and had been very generous with certain charities. He seemed to have made contributions that put him in favor with the chief, and Jennings might have been running for office if all these molestation accusations had not surfaced. The three officers agreed that they had better conduct this investigation thoroughly.

The more senior detective from the earlier questioning of Matt was placed in charge of the case. Henry Pailof was white, about fifty years old with a bit of a paunch, but he still looked fit and was reasonable and patient when he examined people or evidence. His sandy colored hair was thinning, but he was so tall that it wasn't noticeable unless he was seated without his cap on. He chewed a lot of gum and may have been a reformed smoker.

The second officer, Sergeant Parker, was a black woman who had been involved with the Nelsons when they had a home invasion by a mentally ill neighbor who camped in their woods. She remembered them and the house so she was a welcome addition to the team in terms of being up-to-speed on just how unusual was this family. She was no nonsense and stern, military fit, but also knew how to be human and connect with the public. She had been remarkably effective with suspects, often finding a way to get them to give up the truth where other officers had failed.

The third member of the team had recently come over to the State Barracks. He had started out as a 'campus cop' at the university, but got sick of underage beer busts and breaking up parties in violation of COVID 19 restrictions. He wanted to sink his teeth into real detective work and the "Case of the Missing Cobra," as they called it, was as good a place as any for him to begin. The problem with him was that he might be just a bit overzealous in his anxiety to achieve, and he didn't seem to have significant people skills. He was likely to blurt things out or to step right into someone else's work. "Oblivious to others" was what one former supervisor had stated. Officer Robert Winston was as likely to mess something up as he was to uncover needed information. He appeared to be of mixed race which had been a real asset on campus.

The team decided to divide up the work in the following ways: Officers Parker and Winston would go door to door in the neighborhood where the murder had occurred. This was an important assignment as clues and perpetrators are often close to the scene of the crime but also dangerous as the assailant might become combative if he saw a single officer at the door. If there were two of them, even criminals were typically much better behaved. It also allowed one officer to do the questioning while the other used his or her eyes to pick up additional information.

Lt. Pailof would keep coordinating all leads and communicating with the transportation companies who might have information from rides given that day. He also checked with scientists to learn more about the type of snake that might have been involved in this murder. He wanted to know their habits, habitats, and how long they could live if displaced from their preferred environments. In other words, was it possible that a snake of this type could have taken up residence in East Apple, Connecticut? And if so, could it have been living in this older apartment building and come up through the floor boards or the sewer? Or is it possible that someone placed this snake in that apartment hoping it would find human prey?

The last phase of the lieutenant's duties was to determine through forensic and medical science if a human being who happened to have some abnormal snake DNA might be able to produce the quantity and quality of venom which had produced this outcome. Could Grace Nelson have killed Mr. Jennings with her own venom? That is, has such a thing ever happened anywhere in the world?

And so the team began its explorations into the neighborhood, the vegetation, the transportation and the history of deaths due to snake bites. When the team of Parker and Winston reported in that night they had one interesting story that stood out. Apparently three separate residents of the area had reported seeing a little old lady being pushed by a young boy in the vicinity of Jennings' apartment. In one case the viewer said that the old lady was carrying a cat, but neither of the others reported anything like that. The cat didn't really seem relevant, and none of them could guess how a cat could be confused with a snake, still it was an interesting tale.

Other than this pair of folks, nothing out of the ordinary was reported by anyone. There was a guy who eventually confessed that he kept a pet duck in his bathtub, but he swore he never abused the animal and would be letting it go on the next clear day when he'd get over to a lake. He seemed harmless enough even if a little low on feathers or something 'upstairs' himself, but there was no way to connect the duck, or this pursuit of a pet, to the snake attack. In fact, two people wished they did have a 'house snake' as the apartment complex was apparently overrun with mice half the year. Clearly the murdering critter had been new to the scene.

But two major lines of inquiry were introduced: where was the snake now, and didn't Mr. Jennings have a girlfriend who had just started paying for his upkeep? Had anyone questioned her and did she, perhaps, keep snakes?

As she was known to be wealthy, but a female, the Lieutenant took Sergeant Parker with him to go interview the 'grieving' significant other while Officer Winston was sent to look for any signs of the snake. Parker and Pailof found the friend of Jennings just as she was about to have a late lunch. She went by the name Mrs. Kay as Kay was the last name of her late husband who had invented some kind of gadget for dishwashers, thus the money came in from his patent.

They were invited to watch her eat while they asked their questions. Initially it appeared that she had been expecting company, so lavish was the repast, but it was soon obvious that Mrs. Kay enjoyed a hearty appetite rivaled by few others. She commenced with a large glass of fruit juice out of which she noisily gulped and then sucked on the rind of the orange garnee. This was barely consumed before her fingers were in a soft cheese dip as her cracker had broken, so she assisted each morsel to her mouth not only with her fingers, but by even licking under her nails!

Having been raised to be lady-like, it was difficult for Sergeant Parker to look at Mrs. Kay while she ate, never mind when she would respond to their questions while masticating large quantities of ham, bread and boiled eggs. When she got to the layer cake and grapes, it was also making the Lieutenant weak in the knees to watch their subject chomp. In any case they managed to understand that she had learned about Mr. Jennings from a friend who hung around another jailed man because she had a crush on him. Mrs. Kay was lonely with plenty of money and decided she would like to 'sponsor' a fellow in need especially if he had a good sexual appetite. Then she laughed stating that she "had plenty of appetites". So she bailed the guy out, out of the 'kindness of her heart' and felt terrible that he died and in such a gruesome way. They left feeling quite convinced that Mrs. Kay knew nothing more and was only murderous to a good lamb chop.

On the other hand, Officer Winston was so excited to have a detective mission all on his own, that he brought along a team of CSI's so he would have others to direct. Apparently, when a snake slithers across an old polished floor as one had done at Jennings' apartment, the floor grabs onto a few scales from the skin and a trail is laid out which can identify the width and probable length of the snake. A scale then provides DNA which can also be analyzed to determine the exact type of snake involved. As to where the snake had gone, it seemed it had appeared in the room as though carried, and had disappeared at the front doorway, as though carried again!

31

NOSEY NEIGHBORS

One neighbor called Lieutenant Pailof the day after his officers had made their rounds through his apartment complex. He said he had not thought much about it at the time, but the more he conjured up the scene in his mind, the more he felt certain that the two people he had reported seeing were probably kids in costumes. He said he could remember dressing up like that with his cousin when he was a kid, and if they had a wheelchair at the time she could have passed for an old lady or a boy and he could have been either as well. "You see," he added, "that person in the wheelchair was so camouflaged that it could have been most anyone, large or small, sitting there under the blanket. No actual skin was showing and that thick hair could have been a wig."

Pailof thanked him for an interesting perspective and said that they would consider this possibility. Once he hung up the phone, he scratched his chin and muttered "Maybe there is a way you guys, rather than no fucking way." He was thinking of the comments Dr. Nelson had made in anger, but the man's daughter, Grace, might not be as sweet a child as her dad wanted to think. Maybe she was even capable of a revenge murder.

But when Winston came in with his report the lieutenant had to consider the matter yet again. He had evidence that a six foot long Cobra had slithered through Jennings' apartment and had most likely been carried in by someone. It was hard to see just how this would jibe with Grace. The lieutenant made his officer lay out every detail, but the DNA evidence screamed loudly that this was an actual snake with strong venom. On the other hand he did consider the report of the neighbor regarding 'kids in costumes' to have some merit.

Slowly he began to consider the possibility that maybe both things were possible; that a snake might have committed the brutal bite, but those who carried it in might well have been a couple of kids in costumes and using a wheelchair.

He arranged for himself and Sergeant Parker, who already had established rapport with the family, to go visit the Nelsons that evening. A few more questions wouldn't do any harm and maybe they could shake somebody up enough to provide something of use. "One can always dream," he muttered to himself.

Matt arrived home at four pm knowing the police were expected by 4:30. It was a pleasant evening and the family sat on lawn chairs arranged in a semi-circle in front of the main barn. When the officers arrived Scruffy was the first one to greet them. The family then rose and asked if they would care for iced tea while they asked their questions. The tea was declined but the police pulled up lawn chairs right next to Grace. They asked her to tell the story again of how she returned to life in the cellar.

Grace said, "Although I was dead at the time, I believe that the Goliath spiders came to the upper cemetery where I was buried and dug until my coffin was freed. Then, as a team, they managed to drag me down the hill and kind of bounced my casket down the cellar stairs and into the basement of this house where they lived or had lived."

"With all that movement including bumps I was somehow awakened, but I could see nothing but black. I mean it was so dark that nothing was actually seeable, all was dark. I dozed off and on for a number of days, maybe weeks. Then something else happened, and I could see a speck of light through one corner of the box. Then I would sleep again. Finally, I think I moved and scared a snake that had entered my coffin seeking a dry place in that wet cellar. Its fear led it to bite me, but for reasons I can't understand I didn't die. A friend of mine had said I would 'live again' after the spider bites, but that I would be dormant for seventeen years. Now, with the snake bite the combination of venoms in my system somehow woke me up. That's about all I know."

The officers thanked her for that. They then moved on with their questions. Eventually they asked if she ever felt that she was part snake.

"No," she laughed, "I don't even care much for snakes. I feel like a girl."

"But you know your DNA carries both markers of snakes and spiders, don't you?"

"Yes," replied Grace, "But obviously I am more person than critter, just look at me. Being a person is certainly dominant."

"Of course, Grace," said Officer Pailof, "It is just with an unusual cause of death we are looking for an unusual assailant. Why, even one of the neighbors reported seeing what he thought were two kids hanging around Mr. Jennings' apartment maybe wearing costumes, and one was riding in a wheelchair. Now that's some theory isn't it? That the snake was transported to the victim's house by two kids!"

Grace looked pale; she twisted her hands in her lap. All she could say was, "I guess." And she didn't make eye contact with anyone.

Now the officers stood up. Sergeant Parker stated that they had enough questions and probable cause to ask a judge for a warrant to search the premises. Did the Nelsons want them to go through this formal step or would they let them get on with a search of the home and outbuildings right then and there?

It looked to Matt like Elena Maria was about to say "Okay, go ahead," but he saw some fear pass over Grace's face like a swarm of gnats. Matt quickly interjected, "It's not that we want to put you through extra trouble, but I'd just kind of like to get my house in order before anyone else goes through it; and I hope that you and your staff won't destroy the place while you are searching for your snake."

With that the troopers took their leave saying that they would return with the warrant in a day or two. Elena Maria asked Matt what that was all about and he said, "Maybe Grace has something to say?"

Grace said, "No, I have nothing to say, I just feel awkward having them go through my underwear drawer."

With that remark Matt laughed. But he also recalled that the look on her face had appeared more frightened than annoyed. He believed that Grace had something to hide. In any case, if she was smart, whatever it was would disappear before those officers could return.

Trying to appear nonchalant, Grace spent much of the day reviewing the places she had stored the clothing that made up their disguises. The one thing she worried about was the wheelchair as the police had mentioned it on multiple occasions. She figured anyone could have a wig, or old ragged clothing, but the wheelchair might somehow be identifiable. Plus any of the clothing she was worried about she had shredded and buried out at the edge of the land abutting the barn. This area was mostly under a canopy of blackberry and raspberry bushes and no one would want to get torn up searching under those branches.

Finally, in desperation, she went to speak with her dad and asked Matt if he would get rid of the old wheelchair in the attic just to help keep the police from getting too excited about nothing. He asked if that would mean a lot to her and when she said "Yes" he said, "Okay, I'll meet you upstairs. Bring my toolbox and a garbage bag." He asked no other questions.

Things were looking good from Grace's perspective. Her "house was in order" and she knew her dad was a true ally. If only the State Police hadn't been so speedy and efficient, but apparently they had asked the prosecutor's office if they could rush the search warrant through to the judge. They were a little afraid that some of the evidence might go missing if they delayed the search. Just as Matt was walking to his pickup truck with an armload of old wheelchair parts, the police arrived with their warrant.

32

DAD'S SACRIFICE

"Under the circumstances we hope you won't mind if we ask to have a look in that bag you are carrying, Dr. Nelson?" and the officer stated Matt's name with a slight hint of a sneer crossing his face.

Matt was a good psychologist, and he wanted to be certain not to lose his cool with these folks a second time, especially when they had a warrant to search his home. "Of course not Officer Winston," he said without a trace of returning the rebuff. "I was just loading up a donation to the local soup kitchen. While it is not food, they serve a large number of people with disabilities and welcome this sort of item." He set his armload of wheelchair parts down in front of the officer.

"Looks an awful lot like this turns into a wheelchair" said Winston.

"Oh, it does," said Matt. "If you have any need for it you are welcome to it. It is amazing how fast a house of this size collects family junk."

"Well, let's just set this aside and see how many other things strike the team as relevant. We are hoping to start in your attic and work our way down through the house before we move to the barn."

And so, now feeling the rain from that 'cloud of suspicion' over his head Matt trudged up the two flights of stairs eventually leaving Officer Winston and two other men to look through anything in the attic which caught their attention. As they had entered the house this team all placed plastic bag-like boots over their shoes, what looked like shower caps on their heads, and donned gloves. Their belts held evidence bags of various sizes and metal instruments resembling giant tweezers, plus each carried a small camera. They certainly gave the appearance of taking this assignment seriously.

After about two hours the men descended from the attic to the outside. They placed several bagged items in the back of their van in a lockbox. A quick view of the items seemed to reveal random shirts and a blanket, nothing that disturbed Grace at all, until she saw one wig in a bag. She then wondered if that could prove anything. At any rate the procedure now seemed to be that two officers remained at their house while one went out to pick up coffee. There was a short sort of official coffee break, and then the team resumed work on the second floor of the house.

Here they went immediately to Grace's room and left nothing undisturbed; every drawer was gone through if not dumped out, they looked under her rugs, and behind wall hangings, they felt along the sides of her closet as well as reaching way into the back of its shelves. They even stripped her bed and felt every inch of her pillow, untied her knotted socks and scarves and checked out the soap in her underwear drawer. Grace felt violated and left the room so that she would not act badly.

They gave nearly equal attention to her parents' bedroom especially since apprehending Matt with his garbage bags full of 'contraband'. They seemed to be enjoying exploring their destructive tendencies, but they were probably simply doing an excellent job of searching. Then they went into Elena Maria's closet and really got excited when they discovered it led to a hidden room with a trap door in the floor. They were further amazed that the ladder from this door led down, not to the first floor, but directly to the basement. Of course that was the basement that officially had an old woman and her son buried in it and of which there had been so many stories. And among the strangest stories was the one of Grace returning to life down there due to some weird interactions between snake and spider venom. "I wonder," said one of the investigators, "how these people can live with a kid who they know has been dead, buried, and brought back to life? Do they think about it like now it's time to kiss the corpse good night?"

Even Winston had the sense to tell this guy to knock that talk off while he was in this house; that it was unprofessional and ungentlemanly given his position. That shut him up as it sounded too much like 'write-up' language. But this is how they were thinking as they continued the assignment at the farmhouse on Cemetery Hill Road.

The first floor was also filled with curiosities. Only a few trunks and the insides of books seemed to really raise interest. Although the warrant stated they sought clothing or costumes possibly connected to a criminal investigation, they seemed to think that something important to them could be stuffed into the pages of books. They might have found a couple dusty bookmarks and four-leaf clovers but little else: No secret letters from beyond and no death threats to Jennings.

The large portrait in the parlor held their interest for a few minutes as the papers had once described it as having "other worldly" qualities. They took it down from the wall and felt along its backing, but then returned it to its place. It would be pretty hard to justify pulling it apart in the search for a costume or a snake. They were probably wise not to mess too much with an item that might exhibit a mind of its own and which, unbeknownst to them, was the father of the child they most suspected of conjuring up a snake to kill Mr. Jennings. Jennings had done harm to Grace, and she was only defending herself and Katie, but these officers did not know the whole story, only vague speculations. That portrait on the wall knew more than did they and more than anyone in this household would have thought to give him credit.

The portrait had sat on the wall in this house off and on since the 1880s. His knowledge was mostly a curse to him but had allowed him to make a few necessary interventions on the family's behalf. He had also acted on impulse once, which was how he had fathered Grace, but that is another story. Today he rests upon the wall keeping a watchful eye on all and hoping he will not be needed again. Currently, he has suspicions that Grace may be in enough trouble that she will need him, but since she came back to life this time, she has not.

The investigators again carry out their evidence bags bearing labels for where each item has been found. They lock and store the items in the van locker. They make a final trip into the cellar which does not hold many items in which to store contraband, since they choose not to dig up the two marked graves, and they are finally finished with the house.

They divide up the barns and other out buildings. Their methods are more visual here, basically a walk through to be certain nothing grossly suspicious is overlooked. Then they each take metal detectors and walk an assigned section of the yard. There are a few stops where nails or old horseshoes are unearthed, but nothing appears to contain a weapon or a snake cage. They are just completing a walk around the perimeter of the yard proper when Scruffy, who has been following them intermittently, decides to begin digging under some heavy branches. He quickly unearths a plastic bag and inside that bag they find some children's clothing which has been shredded; recently shredded if their eyes are correct. It even looks to have been a boy's shirt and pants. The dog won't leave the pants alone as they seem to contain a food stain which he finds attractive.

The investigators add these items to the bags in their vehicle. They then confer with each other and seek out Dr. Nelson with whom they share the information that they must take Grace along to the station and either he or his wife may join her. Matt surprises them by stating that, "Anything suspicious they have encountered is his doing, and he will gladly go in for questioning but they should leave the child alone."

"What do you know about the snake?" Winston inquires.

"I found the snake at the University," says Matt. It was in a biology exhibit and I removed it to get revenge on this man who so badly hurt Grace, Jennings' own daughter Katie, and who has frightened us all. I carried the snake in a sack into Jennings' apartment and I left it there after slinging it into his lap. I had intended that no one should be accused of this because I rid the world of a cruel and perverted man, but you folks have been too much for me." And Matt extended his wrists to be handcuffed.

33

BAIL OUT

A ll Grace could think about was that her daddy had gone to jail in order to protect her. She knew what had really happened, and he had not brought a snake into Jennings' apartment, she had; and she was that snake. Was there any way to save her dad without incriminating herself and also getting Katie in trouble? She wished she could talk to her mother, but knew Elena Maria was overwhelmed with caring for the baby, worrying about Matt, and preparing for another birth. Elena Maria even had a call in to her parents asking them to please visit and give them a hand.

Grace was happy that her grandparents were coming, but still could think of nothing but her dad. She wondered if any part of her mother thought that perhaps Matt had committed this crime in order to rid the world of a terrible menace. She felt fearful of asking that, but also wanted to reassure her mom of his innocence. Maybe her grandparents could help with this discussion.

Then Elena Maria came to see Grace. She reported that their family lawyer had assured her that she could get Matt out on bail although it would be a large bond. That meant a lot of money which guaranteed that he would not skip town to avoid court. The reason they could get him out even though this was a murder charge was because he had no prior record, he was cooperating with the authorities, his act could be considered "justifiable homicide", and he had deep roots in the community.

Still, Elena Maria had to explain that they would have to be very careful with money for a while because the University was putting Matt on a paid suspension which might turn into a full suspension if he were to be found guilty. The University had to be very certain about the integrity of its faculty and certainly a crime like this was crossing that line.

Grace felt herself fading to a paler shade of ash than her skin had already been. Yes it was great to get dad out of jail, but now he might be forfeiting the career he had worked for so hard. The lie didn't seem worth it for the family. She paced the floors and had the urge to hit her head against a mantle, but she did not. She tried to play with baby Mattie although he only wanted to sleep. She asked if she could peel vegetables for dinner, however Elena Maria wasn't organized enough to even know what she was serving that night as it was so rare not to have Matt involved with that meal. In short, Grace could hardly contain her anxiety as she lived with this horrible lie her father had taken on to protect her.

Then she thought of Katie; what must she be going through living next door with her father so recently dead, and knowing that she had played a role in his loss. Their whole household must be gloomy and sad. Where was their next paycheck coming from and who would help them carry away his unwanted things or even bring the trash to the street? Small matters in the grander scheme of things, but sad each time they came up against an item that their dad used to handle.

It was some two hours later when the Nelson family attorney made a second call. It seemed the bail was being refused because they could not hold Matt, the charges would not stick. He not only flunked the lie detector test when he was trying to take responsibility for the crime, but someone from the University of Connecticut herpetology laboratory had come forward: There was no missing snake, the lab's census was carefully taken each week and no snakes were missing or unaccounted for. Matt might be in trouble for interfering with an investigation, but he was no longer under arrest. Elena Maria was directed to go pick her husband up as soon as possible.

However, this change was not necessarily good news as the officers maintained their original suspicion that Grace had committed this crime, and she would be wanted for further questioning. The attorney hastened to add if she did go in for this questioning then she, the attorney, wanted to be present in order to protect her and insure that she would absolutely be tried as a juvenile. First, her age was very young, and she had been molested by this subhuman who had taken advantage of her fragile situation. She believed she could protect Grace from ever having to serve time. What she did not realize was how Grace had arranged to get a snake into Jennings' apartment. What the lawyer assumed was a charge for transporting a dangerous animal for the purpose of committing a misdemeanor or a felony was in fact, committing a felony using her own body or means, such as when a prizefighter might knowingly strike a person a blow with his own lethal force. In other words, both a prizefighter and Grace could become lethal weapons.

Grace's head felt like a gyroscope; whichever way she turned it, her brain produced unexpected and odd shapes and colors. She knew everyone would want answers from her and she did not know if she should trust others or if she needed a great story to cover her tracks, or slither marks in this case. And, of course, there was also Katie to be considered. How much longer could she stand the pressure of the lie versus the reality of being implicated in the crime by telling the truth? What a dilemma, and with dad coming home soon she had better get her story straight.

She told her mother that she wasn't feeling too well, which was the truth, and that she wanted to lie down for a little nap, then she went to her room and pulled the covers over her head. For a few minutes her mind stayed in turmoil resisting the sleep that would give her a little peace, but then she fell into a deep slumber.

While sleeping, her body decided to seek safety in a shift. It began at the tips of her toes as her feet blended together and then it felt as though she was being placed inside of a slimy sheaf as a coating of scales moved its way up her body from the toes to her hips and then along her torso and arms. If she had awakened at that moment she would have felt that she was bound by a straightjacket, but she slept through the transformation until the scales covered her entire body including her arms, head and hair. Yet, Grace slept on.

It seemed the police ended up bringing Matt home as they wanted a few more words with Grace, and were likely trying to avoid her attorney for as long as possible. Elena Marie was glad to have Matt home as she did find it stressful to manage Grace, pack up Mattie, and drive out there, so without thinking it through she welcomed the delivery and allowed the officer in. The officer asked where Grace was and Elena Maria said she was tired and had gone to bed. Then she turned to her husband and while Matt was greeting her and attempting to explain all he had learned, Officer Winston bounded up the stairs to Grace's bedroom.

He saw her shape in the bed and called her name. She was so asleep that she did not move. He stepped right up to the bed and gave her blankets a good poke. She started to roll a bit to release herself from these quilts, but the snake was excellent at sensing danger. As she finished unrolling, her tongue was rapidly darting out of her mouth, and her lower half was starting to form a coil. When Winston began to realize just what he was messing with it was already too late for him to pull back. His hesitation due to pure shock and terror, and the snake's extreme speed when threatened, led to a fatal confrontation for the young officer. He was bitten on the neck and left staggering for breath before he even had an opportunity to call out for help.

Grace was then able to comprehend what her body had done as a snake. She too was horrified and she collapsed back into the pile of sheets, blankets and quilts while the policeman slid down her wall as he collapsed to the floor no longer breathing. His body turned over a chair as it slipped down and the crash was loud enough to bring her anxious father up the stairs.

He took the officer's pulse and finding none quickly wished to aid his poor daughter whom he prayed had not been injured. But when he pulled back the bed covers she was just sleeping peacefully and seemed a bit dazed to be awakened. This quickly turned to joy at seeing her dad home again, and then terror at the sight of the body in blue.

Grace appeared to be herself again and was very confused about the officer. Matt was aghast as he began to comprehend what had just occurred, and he really did not want poor pregnant Elena Maria to have to deal with this.

34

LET THERE BE LIFE

F ather and daughter quickly made a decision to hide the officer's body, not for long, not buried in the cellar with Emily and Will, but just long enough to absorb what had transpired. Matt also wanted to be able to conceal the death from Elena Maria at least until they could think of a way to tell her that did not include the phrase "Your daughter can turn into a snake."

Matt sat on the bed with Grace until she had a chance to describe this shape-shifting thing that took her over. She explained how it was that a snake had killed Mr. Jennings as it was really Grace taken over by her snake blood. And today's accident just happened because she had been so worried about her father and had not been able to sleep. "Just think," she sobbed, "If mother had come upstairs to wake me up and the snake had attacked her? I cannot live with myself like this. I can't control the shifts and I don't want to be a murderer!"

Matt was crying too. Softly he said, "I don't want you killing people either, and we don't want you in trouble. How can we fix this?"

Then Grace jumped out of bed. "Maybe he hasn't been dead too long, maybe there is a way my father, the portal guide, can bring him back? Maybe there is a way for that father to help me in a different way this time. Maybe he can save me and let me live because I love it here with this family!" And Grace ran downstairs and into the parlor.

She had not spoken to her father nor really looked at him since she had returned to life this time. She had hoped that by by-passing any relationship with him she could maintain a normal life and not need his powers which she considered both good and evil. But there he sat on the wall looking both handsome and remote as though he knew nothing of what went on in this house or of the forces controlling his biological daughter. He was detached and asked for nothing from her. And most of his last acts on her behalf had been to protect the world from her. She could not forget the harshness of his touch when she had behaved badly. All she could do now was pray he saw the good side of her and that he would act to support her mortality now that she behaved with caring and had learned to love others.

In a panic she fell before the painting and began an intense litany of begging for help saying that she needed it quickly while there might still be time. Deep within the painting Ben heard her plea and felt a compassion that he had blocked for many years. She was saying that a young man lay dead upstairs and that the snake who took over her body had killed this man. Further, that he was a policeman and if she did not act fast it would be beyond hopeless, and the State would be within their rights to put her to death for committing this crime. Please could he just bring back this man before his body grew cold and his mind would be tainted by death, were the words he heard her saying.

Then the portrait answered with a deep "Bring him to me."

Grace was back up stairs in a flash. She asked her father to quickly bring the officer down to the portrait and she would make sure her mother was occupied elsewhere. Matt loaded the dead man, whose weight seemed extremely heavy in his limp state, into his arms and made his way to the parlor. Grace flew into the kitchen and saw her mother tenderly bathing Mattie. "We'll be with you in just a few minutes," said Grace. Then she was off to join her father.

And so, the father and daughter team of Grace and Matt stood watch over the officer as her father in the portrait made a few deep indescribable sounds. Then Officer Winston began to stir and groan a little. He was helped onto the couch by Matt, and Grace brought him a glass of water.

"What happened?" Officer Winston said. "I feel like I got hit by a bucket loader. My head hurts and I had the weirdest dream."

"We aren't sure," said Matt. "While I was kissing my wife hello you seemed to rush upstairs to speak with Grace, but the first thing she knew was when a chair fell over in her room, she opened her eyes and you were lying on the floor like a pile of dirty laundry. When she couldn't rouse you she yelled down to us and I found you there unconscious. I carried you down here thinking it would be easier when the ambulance arrived, but just as I went to call them you woke up. If it was only a dizzy spell I wasn't certain if you would want to go to the hospital or not?"

"God, no," said Winston. "I don't want all the guys at the station making fun of me for passing out on the job."

"Well," Matt added, "You should probably get your blood pressure checked at some point if this was associated with running up the stairs too fast. Then, what was your dream about?"

"I think I've been too intensely absorbed in snakes lately," he responded. "I dreamed I had walked into Grace's room, but instead of a girl in her bed there was a giant cobra, and it reeled up at me and then lunged. It bit me somewhere; I'm not sure where because in the dream, that was when I passed out. Then it felt like I was rolling down a very long tunnel, just tumbling over and over again when suddenly I started to move backwards like I was in an old movie and someone was rewinding. Then I woke up with this wicked headache and I'm lying here in your parlor."

"It must have felt awful," said Grace. She appeared kind and genuine offering to get anything the officer needed. But the policeman decided he was feeling much better although he would question Grace on another day. For the moment he thought it would be more effective if he went back to the barracks to communicate with the team. And so he was escorted to the door by Matt who wished him well.

Matt sent Grace back upstairs to get ready for dinner while he helped Elena Maria finish her duties with Mattie and to get the meal on the table. After dinner he suggested that once Mattie was in bed they should have a family conference. Elena Maria looked quizzically at Matt but asked nothing; Grace looked at the floor knowing that he wanted her to tell her mother about the problems with the shape shifting. She hoped her mom could take it, and did have some hope as Elena Maria had learned many strange and really supernatural things since moving into this house. She did not want this fact to move them far apart again.

After dinner was over and the dishes done, Grace slowly began the description of her first shape shift when she had wanted to be a snake and put an end to Mr. Jennings but how it had taken an unexpected turn. Grace could not get the snake to form, but instead became her arachnid side and was injured by Mr. Jennings.

She went through all the descriptions of shifting including fatally attacking Mr. Jennings and accidentally biting the officer that very afternoon. She hastened to add all the reasons Mr. Jennings deserved such harsh treatment, but stated clearly that today's incident frightened her, not because she couldn't predict which creature she would become, but because she hadn't anticipated becoming a creature at all. She ended with a heart rending plea for any ideas that might get rid of this curse that caused a snake to take over her body.

Elena Maria did not rebuff her child. She reached out and took Grace in her arms. She rocked from side to side for a few moments as though to comfort them both. Then she let Grace go and pulled back a little. "There is only one suggestion I can make and it worked when I needed it, but it always comes with a price. Go again to the portal and ask to be set free of this curse. Ask to be a normal girl, the way he always wanted you to be, a girl who is free from magic or curses."

35

ARRIVALS

Before Grace could find the words she wanted to use with her father at the portal, her grandparents arrived. They had feared that Matt was still being held by the police and had no idea of what had actually transpired in the house. Learning that Grace might be in trouble with the authorities was not a surprise, but when they heard what her actual problem was, and that she needed to have the snake in her DNA controlled, they felt nothing but fear and sympathy for the poor child. Nonna had been through enough with "the portal" that she even feared for the girl having to request help from him although she knew it was necessary under these awful circumstances. Nonna also suspected that a part of Benjamin still cared very much for this child, so maybe his help would not come at too dear a price. They were certainly all hoping for a good outcome.

If the 'uncontrollable snake issue' were to be remedied then the only major problem which Grace would still have to face would be that of convincing the police that she had done no wrong. That might be almost as challenging as getting the snake out of her system as

Officer Winston had found actual slither prints on the floors in the Jennings' apartment. He would be difficult to convince of Grace's innocence. The possibility that a snake got into the apartment on its own seemed impossible to him because of the markings he had found. The officers had the tire prints of the wheelchair, and Matt had been caught transporting its parts away from the home. Yet, since the father was not to blame for bringing the snake to Jennings, from what did he think he was protecting his daughter? Why did he state that the snake was one he had stolen when he had not, in fact, stolen a snake? Clearly, he must know that Grace was responsible.

There was still a lot of explaining to do by both the father and the daughter. The police were also not certain of the role Katie Jennings might have played in her father's murder, although she too had been molested by him. They weren't certain if her action in assisting Grace had been one that was justifiable. Her dad's brutality which had nearly killed her might make a jury very sympathetic; or would they view Katie's behavior as criminal given the deadly outcome. The police also could not be certain which one of the girls had actually placed the snake in Katie's father's apartment. Perhaps Katie had been assisted by Grace rather than the other way around. Was a snake even something that two little girls would handle? And if so, how did they manage a venomous snake when apparently a grown man could not?

And so Grace and her extended family now braced for a battle that could set Grace free from this pain and worry or leave her in deep trouble both at the mercy of something within her body and also from the force of the law. After a good breakfast, for what else could her nonna suggest, Grace entered the parlor and sat across from the portrait of her biological father. She did it alone knowing that those who loved her were close-by. She feared that bringing them all into the room might seem to challenge her father, and really he held all the cards.

Grace began by saying she was there for two reasons: first, she must thank him for coming to her rescue when she might have accidentally killed a police officer and so badly wanted him to live; and second because she needed one more favor and then she promised she would ask for nothing else. She saw the eyes in the portrait move towards her but no words were spoken. She continued to explain her situation.

"You know I was buried up the hill in the cemetery for a short time. And the immediate cause of my death was poison excreted by the Giant Goliath Bird Eating Spiders which I allowed to bite my wrists. Old Emily in the cellar had promised me that in so doing I would insure the ability to arise again in about seventeen years which was what the spiders and other large bugs did after a period of dormancy. Other than that it seemed certain that you would end my life for the wicked acts I had started performing. I even would have hurt precious little Mattie if I had not been stopped. I admit there was an evil in me which I can neither explain nor understand."

"However, once I was bitten and went into dormancy, my brain continued to work, and it was fighting this decision; it did not want me to lie around for seventeen years; it wanted me to escape death. Then the giant spiders came in the night and dug up my coffin and dragged it home to this house. I woke up again in the cellar just beneath you, but I was still dormant except for my brain, and sometimes my diaphragm and throat could work a little. Each time I tried to think of a way to escape I just became overwhelmed and passed back into unconsciousness. Time went by, I do not know how much, but when I awoke this particular time things smelled very damp, and there was a crack in the corner of my coffin which a snake was using to join me in my box."

"I was horrified to look down at myself, unable to move, and see this creature slithering across my body. Then the most frightening and unimaginably horrible thing happened, it bit me! I again passed out; however, when I awakened I was filled with strength and felt alive. My muscles were twitching; my brain was thinking in many directions and my legs wanted to run. I was so alive that I had to get out of that box."

"Eventually I used my shoe and wedged my way out. I was determined to hide from everyone in the house and just sort of live in shadows in the basement, but my human needs were too strong, and I was compelled to find food which eventually led to my being discovered. But the main concern I now have is that snake and arachnid are part of my DNA; such a part of me that, without wishing it, I apparently may turn into either one of these, spider or snake, if I am anxious or too tired. While initially this seemed like a strength it has become a burden, a most dangerous burden and something which I must be rid of or learn to control without error. If you really want me to live a normal human life, and I am in a wonderful family; then please, please help me to just be human."

"My whole existence has seemed cursed, and you are my last hope to reverse this curse. I thank you for originally giving me life, and now I wish to be fully human and deal with life as all humans must; just please take the creatures out of me even though it means I must age and eventually decay like everyone else."

Then the portal spoke and his deep voice was unmistakably from far away. "All humans will eventually decay and perish as you aptly describe, but those of us in the portal never die nor do we truly live, we are in a state of limbo and only react when we are called upon. I am doomed to go on forever grieving and suffering and never leaving this earth, and I am more miserable than are you. But my fate was sealed during that cursed War Between the States when brother killed brother and blood drenched the ground. I tried to live so that I might return to your mother, but it was not meant to be so I lived, but could never truly return to her, and some of that might be because of the horror of my deeds as I tried to stay alive during that hellish time."

He added, "I owe it to you to help you, and I owe it to Victoria too. I shall find a way to do as you ask, but then I shall need a very big favor in return, one that will change things for all time forward. If I take away the influence of the Goliath Spiders and the snake, will you promise to follow through on my request no matter how strange it may seem?"

And Grace felt a rush of relief and hope. She replied, "Anything you want papa, anything." So the next step of her journey was about to unfold.

36

THE CURE

Grace had a smile on her face which reflected her new feeling of true happiness. Her father had promised to see that she was freed from the influence of the bites she had received from both the giant spiders and the snake. While these creatures had contributed to saving her life or resurrecting her, depending on how you looked at it, Grace could not deal with the consequences of having this DNA coursing through her body. It could suddenly affect how she would appear and behave. She did not want to randomly become anything but herself at any given time.

He had cautioned her that this meant she would no longer have the power that the arachnid and the reptile held within their bodies, but this was okay with her, she would rather rely upon herself and use rational human methods of protection. She did wonder when the transformation would occur, or if it had already, but thus far she had no outward sign. She thought of getting really aggravated by something to see if the creatures were within her, but she feared their return enough to not welcome this test. Perhaps if she experienced no actual signs or signals over time, that would be her evidence.

Then she recalled that there was a second phase of this agreement; she must do a favor for her father and as of yet he had not described what this was to be. Would he cure her before he got his reward or would she need to render services prior to receiving his help? She decided that today was a good day to broach that question.

Grace entered the parlor and was pleased that no one else was about. With her nonna and grandfather visiting it was sometimes hard to find an empty room although the house was large. She knew it was best to approach her father when they were alone, better concentration for his deep journeys. She sat in the chair across from the portrait and began by saying, "I am here father." Then she waited.

After only a few moments Benjamin's face appeared alive and he greeted her in return. Then he said, "I expect you have some questions for me. The first thing I can tell you is that you are cleared of all the venoms; your DNA no longer contains remnants of either snake or spider. In fact, it was replaced with DNA from your adoptive parents so that you may heretofore claim each other as kin, although they are more closely aligned with cousins than as full biological parents. Victoria and I will continue to occupy most of your genes."

"I am so happy, papa. Although I have no idea how this was done, I appreciate it so much. And I know I owe a favor to you. One which you have said would be challenging but very important to you. I am ready to fulfill my debt and anxious to do so. Please tell me what you require," said Grace.

"This will not be easy," said the man in the portrait, "but it will be the last thing that I am ever able to ask of you if it takes place as anticipated. I would like you to take this portrait off the wall and incinerate it in a huge intense fire so that the contents and the frame are burned into oblivion, blasted away, barely any dust should remain. Then I shall truly be free of this life and transported to eternity."

"While I will miss your handsome face, father," Grace said, "I do not fear this task as I am certain I can accomplish this and it won't be too hard. I may require assistance to carry the portrait outside but I can read on the internet how the actual conflagration should be accomplished. Do not fear, I will manage this task for you."

"Ah, Grace," said the portrait, "unfortunately there is another facet to this request which may trouble you emotionally and which will present some difficulties, but which is essential to my eternal happiness. I am sorry to have to ask this of you but I must. Grace, human hair has the potential to last many decades. When a woman has had long thick hair it is not unlikely that some will remain on her head although her skull is otherwise barren of flesh. The hair is simply draped around her skull as a strange adornment to the skeleton. It is a bit like seeing a barn that is falling-in yet it has a good roof."

"I wish to have a lock of your mother's hair. Victoria had such lovely thick hair, often braided and wrapped around her head. It would not only give me pleasure to see her hair again, but if you will be kind enough to burn the hair with my portrait, then I know she and I will be in communication in eternity and I shall cease to be so lonely. Do you think you can do this for me Grace? Dig up your mother's body?"

Grace gasped. This was the furthest thought from her realm of expectations. As kids often say she 'wouldn't have thought of this in a million years' but here was the request. She had often wished that she could see her mother again, but she had imagined the woman she had known as a child, the pretty woman who gave birth to her and cooked special dinners and fretted over her when she was acting wild. It never occurred to her to see her mother as old bones with what would probably look like a wig remaining on her head. She visibly shivered and pulled her shoulders up close to her head.

Finally Grace was able to speak. "This request is as strange to me as if you had asked me to go back in time and join you in fighting during the Civil War, although I understand that would be worse, somehow. But strange or not I cannot deny you after all you have done for me, and I pray my mother will also find this connection welcome. I don't know how I will manage it or when, but I shall do it."

And so Grace left the parlor after learning what the portal had done with her request, and what he wished for in return. She knew that she was now free of the animal spirits within her and that she had an unusual task to perform for her father to repay his efforts. Grace would need to walk around a bit and let the discussion filter through her brain before she could accept the duty fully and conceive of an action plan to perform it. She told her family that she and Scruffy would go for a little walk. They preferred that she not go out alone, but the dog seemed to make them consider her safe.

She and Scruffy had not conceived of a three mile walk, but that was how much they actually did before realizing that they were at the cemetery on the top of Cemetery Hill Road. This was where Grace had been buried and dug up by the spiders, and this was the location of the graves of her legal parents Theodor (Teddy) and Victoria Mills who had perished only a few years apart. Victoria was also her biological mother. Her dad (Teddy) had died in 1905 at the age of sixty-six which was a fairly old age in those days, and her mother had died in 1909 at the age of seventy. That meant that Grace would be exhuming a corpse to cut or steal its hair after it had lain in the coffin for one hundred and twelve years. That seemed like a long time to have been allowed to rest in peace only to be disturbed by your youngest daughter for a haircut. Grace hoped that Victoria would forgive her.

Grace and Scruffy also noted the burial plots of Grace's siblings Jane and Ben the third. They had only been dead since the 1940s but Grace had not been alive after their childhoods so she did not much miss them.

That night Grace fell into a sleep of exhaustion from the long walk and her serious worries. However, at midnight she woke up and told herself it was now or never; that she had to get this horror show over with. She put Scruffy on a leash and dragged a shovel along behind her. Once up the hill she had to rest for several minutes on a collapsed headstone to regain her strength for this mission. Then she felt her way through the graveyard to the place where she had found her mother's marker earlier in the day. Only then did she dare turn on her flashlight to be certain she had the correct grave. She then began to dig finding the old packed down soil very hard to break through, although light to move.

She kept at it for what seemed like hours when she finally felt a clunk that did not sound like stone but a piece of wood. She thought "I must be at the coffin," when suddenly something grasped her ankle. She looked down to see a skeletal hand gripping her foot and trying to pull her into the grave. When she kicked at it with her free foot she lost her balance and was suddenly lying on top of the plot with more of the dirt stirring as though hundreds of dead hands were reaching up for her. Scruffy started barking at these grasping bones and Grace was screaming and beating on them with her fists.

37

THE FOOTBOARD

G race let out a scream that would have turned sweet milk sour it was so desperate. She tried to jump out of bed, but her ankle was caught in some of the carved work on the footboard. She was beginning to wake-up from a nightmare. Her fear was that her lower half might again have turned into a snake, but she was pulling to free her actual foot when both her parents raced in.

"Grace, what is wrong?" they asked together.

She explained that she must have been having a horrible dream. In that dream something had grabbed her foot, and when she went to free herself she became overwhelmed and helpless. Then it felt as though she were a snake again. She was panicky and crying, but they remained and comforted her. Finally, she confided what was actually happening in the dream; that she was trying to exhume Victoria and that the family spirits in the graveyard fought to stop her while attempting to force her to join them. "Gruesome" was all she could say in summary.

Matt said, "That is a very disturbing dream. Do you have any idea what triggered it? You have known that your first mother was in that cemetery for quite some time, just wondering where the terror was coming from now?"

"I didn't want to tell you," said Grace, "because I was afraid you would try and stop me, but I really must honor his request!"

"Wait a minute; slow down kiddo, whose request? Has this got something to do with your bargain with the portrait?"

And Grace said "yes" telling the entire story of the favor to her parents as requested by The Portal.

"Well we can certainly help you to get rid of the painting if that is important to set your dad free," said Elena Maria, "but robbing a grave is another whole matter."

"Yes," said Matt, "we cannot have you risking more trouble with the police when the last situation has still not been resolved. Benjamin must see that he could bring further difficulties into your life."

"But I think," Grace said, "that he only wants to disappear into eternity with my mother and that is all he sees at this point. He is feeling desperate for that connection with her."

"Well, try not to worry about it now," said Matt. "We will figure something out; you get a little rest if you can."

When Matt and Elena Maria sat with her folks a short time later they discussed the predicament. How could Grace honor her father's presumably last request, and still remain on the right side of the law? Her grandfather wondered if they could find some reason to legally exhume Mrs. Mills after all this time. What could they possibly need from her bones that would be a compelling reason to request digging her up after well more than one hundred years? And who were they to the Court to make such a request as Grace would not be acknowledged as Victoria's biological child given the gap in years? They would see that Victoria had long been deceased when it appeared that Grace was born. Regrettably, the legal route did not hold much promise.

"Then we are back to Grace's idea, we must pull off a body snatching" gasped Elena Maria. And they all laughed nervously.

"Actually," said nonno, "We don't have to take the entire body, we just need to get into the grave long enough to cut off a lock of her hair then cover up our digging and get out of there." They all agreed that was a plan. The question remained as to how and when this would be attempted.

"Well by now", nonno said, "the casket will have disintegrated. That means a very small opening is all we would need to get through the dirt and down near the head of the corpse, Victoria that is. I'm just not certain how we cut off a lock of hair and get it back up a pipe. There must be some surgical scissors that can manage this similar to instruments used in robotic surgery. I know just the guy who can help us. He runs a surgical instruments research and development group in Rhode Island and I know he'd set me up with the right tool." With that he left the group to go find his cell phone and place a call.

They waited anxiously and nonno came back to announce he'd be heading for Rhode Island right after lunch. There was a pair of 'periscope scissors,' they called them, that came with a remote controller and could be inserted into a person or area three feet away managing to perform as the remote requested. He could borrow this instrument for tonight, and they only asked that it be returned by the following afternoon. "I guess we raid the tomb tonight," he said feeling like an archeologist on a scientific hunt.

"Did they ask you what you wanted it for," asked nonna?

"They didn't ask, so I let that just slide by me," was his response.

Then some made lunch preparations while others collected dark clothing, gloves, boots, shovels, a plastic baggy for the hair, and, of course, flashlights. Nonno made himself a thermos of coffee to sweeten the car trip and to be certain that he stayed awake for the whole adventure.

When nonno returned from his travels around dinner time they were all ready to feed him and could hardly wait for it to be dark enough so that their adventure could begin. All with the exception of Grace actually, as she was still haunted by the dream she had and the terror of feeling skeletal hands on her ankle bones. Although she had often yearned to see her mother this was not the way for which she had hoped. She also would not be able to explain how she had eventually changed for the better to this person around whom they would be digging. She must not think about the Victoria she had known and loved, but only visualize a very old set of bones that had no memory or personality and only wished to rest in peace. She wasn't digging to see her mother, but only to honor her father's request and allow his life to finally close with a touch of joy that his wife was nearby in eternity.

Grace then raced up to her room to don her dark clothing. Only Elena Maria, who was quite pregnant, and baby Mattie, would stay in the house. It seemed important for the family to stand together as a unit in this mission. They imagined success, but if anything went wrong it seemed important that there were a large number of them perhaps overwhelming those who thought they could handily be stuffed into jail; or perhaps a grave.

The family drove to the top of the hill and disembarked across the street from the cemetery. There were three adults, one child, one dog, three shovels, two front paws and a scissor scope that would be used in the process although Grace and her nonna might do most of the flashlight holding. What they saw in front of them was the hilly shape of the graveyard rising above the road, and bearing predominantly old thin markers. Some were leaning, a few appeared to be pushed down, and among the very oldest the stones were cracked. It was a small plot as cemeteries go, but the citizens buried here had played important roles in the town's history. You could almost feel them waiting for news about local matters; especially in the darkened sky lit only by a cloudy moon.

The team working on this resurrection commenced immediately; the thoughts of this endeavor did not get more pleasant as time passed. The men were excellent diggers, and soon it seemed they were close enough to Victoria to put the pipe in place and to lower the clipping arm. These scissors were attached to a viewing scope so that the surgeon extracting the tumor, or matter, or hair in this case, could examine the object to be excised. When nonno had it in place he asked Grace if she wanted to see her mother's remains, and he warned her there was just hair and bone.

Grace hesitated for a moment and then said she would like to see what she could of her mother. When she peered down the scope her mind played a trick on her, and she was certain that she saw an eye socket wink quickly, and then it was still. There was a good deal of lush hair remaining so Grace knew that the Captain would not be disappointed. She gave the instrument back to her grandfather and he snipped the needed quantity.

As they began to pack up their tools there was a low moan that passed through the cemetery like the sound of a large animal finally giving up in a fight, knowing that it would not live. They all looked around, but seeing nothing, proceeded to the car. Once in the vehicle Scruffy put his head up on Grace and dropped a skeletal hand into her lap. She didn't know what to say so she just patted him and said "Good boy," but her face was green.

38

BLOWING IN THE WIND

When they returned home Grace asked her nonna what she should do with the skeleton's hand Scruffy had given her. Nonna was surprised to see the bones in Grace's possession but said she would put them in a plastic bag and hang it in the barn until morning. In the morning she and nonno would take a walk around the cemetery and see if there were any signs that the dog had disturbed another grave while everyone else was looking for Victoria's hair. She told the child not to give it a second thought, it didn't mean there would be more trouble, and it was just a dog's nature to hunt for bones. But it bothered nonna enough that she did not want those fingers hanging around inside the house.

Then they went in the house, and Matt gave Grace her mother's hair. He said, "I suggest you hang the lock of hair for your father in this bag on the back of his portrait," and he provided her with a clear plastic bag which was zip sealed. "That way," he added, "when we incinerate the portrait we may be certain that they go together.

The only other thing I might suggest is that you keep a little bit of that hair for yourself, after all she was your mom."

Grace became tearful when he spoke those words. "You don't suppose mother will mind?" she asked.

"No," was Matt's response. "Your mother and I know that we did not make you, but we have the gift of raising you and loving you, and that is enough. You should have some keepsake of your biological mother's."

Grace went up to her room where she had a pretty little box that a bottle of perfume had been in. It looked like it was made of black silk, shiny and just a bit ribbed with pearls embellishing the cover of the box. She kept the perfume on her bureau and only saved the box because it was so lovely. Now she had something precious to save inside it. She was tickled. The rest of Victoria's hair was closed in its bag and then taped behind the portrait. Grace whispered to her portrait-dad that Victoria's lock of hair was now his forever. She also confided to him that they would soon take care of the burning which he had requested.

But for now it was late, the "grave robbing" had taken them until close to midnight and children and adults were exhausted. It was time to get some rest and wait until the next day to resolve more issues. Grace went up to bed first, and then one-by-one the adults finished their projects for the night and followed behind her to their bedchambers.

Morning dawned with a clear sky. Bacon and eggs were sizzling in the kitchen and all were cheerfully assembling for the first important meal of the day. Matt had to grab a phone call shortly after 8:30 AM and seemed a bit disconcerted. It appeared that just when so many things were falling into place, the big unresolved issue reemerged;

the police wanted to summon Grace for a conference on what her responsibility had been regarding Mr. Jennings.

The officer also suggested that it might be necessary to question Katie too. They were planning to interrogate each child again with her parent or lawyer present, and then, if necessary, they would question them together. That put an indefinable scent in the air; was the whole house going to burn, not just the portrait, or were there just a few toast scrapings in the sink, and all could be rinsed away? Something was wrong, but how wrong, and how long would it last? Grace's fears gripped her deeply for she had taken a man's life even if she had been a snake at the time.

"Look," said Matt, "it will be several days before the police can gather everyone they need together to make this formal inquiry. Let's continue to do what we need to do and assume we will eventually have our lives back the way we want them. We will just go ahead and take care of your promise to the portrait, and we have a house to get ready for a new baby. Plus, while your grandparents are here we should have a big Italian feast and ask in neighbors who are vaccinated and not afraid to come together. We can't put off good things too long while waiting for life to be perfect. That will never happen, we must just enjoy. So let's go out to the barn and see what we have that might produce the kind of fire your father has requested. Let's have a huge bonfire by the light of the moon and send him off with thanks for his service to this nation and to this family. Let's make it a grand celebration as we know he wants so badly to be free."

Matt's little speech sparked up Grace's enthusiasm. Instead of feeling trapped in never ending problems she felt that their problems were surmountable. She would just have to learn to do things one at a time, take care of a problem, and then move on while having any and all the fun which she could fit into her life. She also realized

CYNTHIA HERBERT-BRUSCHI ADAMS

that her life had begun to improve as soon as she trusted her parents enough to confide all in them.

Her father had called it compartmentalizing when you could put a problem in one stall of the barn and then work in another stall and never worry about the first problem. It was still there but you were not, and you could get ready for this problem when you had to; with luck maybe it would never come up again. That didn't seem likely with this police matter, but Grace was anxious to throw herself into any project she could to avoid thinking about the police and the death of Mr. Jennings.

She asked her mother if the Jennings family could come over when they burned the portrait. Elena Maria said that they could, but only if Grace explained to them first that they were burning this relative's portrait because he had left a request to have this done. She didn't want anyone to think she was maliciously destroying antiques. Then Grace, her nonna, and mother started preparing food. They decided that since the men would be building and tending the fire they could handle the cooking.

The women bought sausage, good Italian bread (no time for baking by hand) chocolates, marshmallows and graham crackers, made a huge salad and baked some ziti with nonna's homemade sauce and grated Parmesan cheese. The wines were always stacked in the cellar so there was really very little work for them to do.

The men hunted around the property for wood that was aged enough to burn well and a safe accelerant that would stimulate the burning, catch everything into the blaze, but not tend to be explosive and create fire where it wasn't intended. Matt thought he had just the thing with some kerosene he's been saving for the right occasion. They also gathered sticks for the marshmallow roasting and then began to set up tables and food stations outside.

Shortly after dark they lit the fire. The plan was to get it extremely hot before the portrait was plunged into its middle. Doing things that way should insure that the portrait, and its attached bundle, would burn totally and completely barely leaving even ash. It would complete the job nearly instantly and thoroughly.

When the time came for the painting to go in, Grace insisted that she should carry at least part of its weight since the request had been made of her. And so she and Matt walked out of the antique house each toting an end of the portrait; they stepped carefully over the granite steps leading out of the house and edged their way toward the fire. They hesitated for a moment each saying a private good-bye and thanks for the miracles wrought by this man, and then they heaved it into the middle of the fire.

The reaction within the fire was as though a giant outdoor movie screen had been ignited. The captain, known as the portal, the portrait, and Grace's father, was enlarged to a near mountainous size as though he had leaped alive into the air and been magnified. He was still in his black military dress uniform; and there, in his arms, was a beautiful young Victoria as she must have appeared on their wedding day. For a moment they laughed and spun around within the center of the fire and then, with a gasp and a moan, they both raised their arms and spun again until they had disappeared into the night air.

39

THE HEARING

Grace felt rather proud after her folks made their spectacular departure together into the sky. She somehow felt more legitimate, more secure; she only wished she could have been born to them as a couple in real times, but that would never be. She had a "real family" now and appreciating them was her top priority: that and taking care of her legal needs, of course.

To that end, she and her dad met with Katie and her mom earlier that day. This evening Katie and her mom would meet with Grace's entire family at their house. They would each have a lawyer with them, and they were preparing for the following day when the meeting took place with the district attorney and some of the officers who had been investigating the case of Mr. Jennings' untimely death. Katie and Grace had to have their story straight and stick together, although Grace repeated to Katie that she would willingly take the responsibility alone since it had been she who had become the murderous snake.

For her part Katie felt nothing but gratitude toward Grace. She believed Grace had saved her from a lifetime of torture by her father, which could otherwise only have been concluded by his death anyway. Katie could sleep again and was even beginning to hum around the house rather than feeling that she should crawl under any object which might hide her. Recently she had spent time fantasizing about a small crack in the paneling near the mantle on their fireplace. She kept wishing that was a sign that she could push a magic button and the paneling would pull back to reveal a secret room. Katie had even decorated that room. It would have a small cozy bed covered in a handmade quilt with matching pillows. There would also be a floor lamp which, when turned on, would illuminate the side of the bed where Katie would wish to read. There were pictures on the walls of sweet, antique dolls and churches, and a built-in bookcase next to the bed was stuffed with great works which Katie had always wanted to read.

Now that her father was gone Katie had ceased dwelling on this fantasy and was instead making her own bedroom look more like that of which she dreamed. She could ask for the things that made her happy and not live in the terror of being molested or even suffocated by the man she was supposed to call "dad." The change brought her personality back to the confident, secure child she had been before her father targeted her little body for his pleasure.

Mrs. Jennings loved the changes in her daughter. She was anxious to have the two girls return to their friendship without the police interference, and to enjoy life now that COVID appeared to be easing up. What she did not know was that Katie and Grace had plotted the murder of her late husband, and that Grace had indeed been the instrument of his demise. It was difficult to know if they must tell her at this meeting, or keep her securely in the dark.

So Mrs. Jennings entered the meeting that evening as the only one present who did not know that Grace could become a viper, or a spider, depending on certain circumstances. But when the lawyers joined them there were then three critical people who were in the dark; and it didn't seem possible for the kids to be represented well if their attorneys were not told the truth. Matt spoke up first saying, "As much as I want to protect my daughter, and as impossible to believe as this information will appear, I must tell all parties concerned with this case that Grace had a curse of sorts that both protected her and made her dangerous. Under certain circumstances she could become a lethal animal in order to protect her own life. And that was just what she had to do to keep Mr. Jennings from fully raping her, and or, her dearest friend, his daughter Katie. Grace turned into a cobra in Mr. Jennings' apartment and intentionally bit him to remove him from harming them again."

"Not only that," Matt continued sounding as he knew the prosecution would, "but Katie Jennings did willfully aid and abet Grace in carrying out this mission as they were both incensed by his behavior which included attempts at murdering each of them. The kids were knowingly and premeditatedly in this together. Can you defend them?"

Mrs. Jennings was covering her mouth with her hand; both attorneys had risen to their feet and were each hanging on to separate sides of the mantel to steady them. There were no questions asked for nearly a minute, when Grace's representative asked Grace, "Can this be true?"

"Yes," she said, "it was true but the ability no longer exists. No matter how hard I try I cannot conjure up a snake or any other creature to take over my life."

"And how many people know that this actually happened?" asked the attorney.

"As my nonna and nonno are in the room it contains every person who knows of my shape-shifting. There are no others who know for certain" Grace said.

"And how many others do you folks know of who suspect that Grace, and or Katie, are responsible for this deed?" the attorney asked again.

Grace answered, "The officer named Winston has found evidence that a snake was in the room because I left slither marks on the rugs and floor, you know, little pieces of scales. But he doesn't know that it wasn't a true snake and that I was the creature. He thinks maybe I carried the snake in to do the murder," said the ten-year-old.

"And have you told ANYONE ELSE?" the attorney queried again.

"No one" said both girls at once.

Then he turned to the parents and grandparents "And have you folks told a single soul about this; friend, cousin; other children? Does anyone else know?"

They all shook their heads affirming that no one else had been privy to this information. "Alright" the lawyer said, "let's be sure that we keep it that way. If we don't tell them I think this is going to be a damn hard hypothesis for them to prove, and I can't imagine a judge or jury that would believe it. It's even better that you cannot do this anymore because you won't be slipping up while we are in court," he concluded.

"So we will lie under oath?" Grace asked in her child's innocent voice?

"With any luck," the lawyer responded, "you won't have to lie; we simply won't introduce the concept of your being able to turn into a snake, so who will ask that question?"

There was head shaking all around the room. "Who, even knowing that Jennings' death was caused by snakebite, would conceive of the possibility that this sweet young woman, child really, would be capable of becoming such a creature?" the lawyer added.

"The only problem I can foresee," said Elena Maria, "is that Grace is on record at the hospital as possessing a small amount of arachnid and snake DNA, but the ability to shape shift would be pure speculation. And as you say, how would a jury ever be convinced that it is possible?"

Then the attorney doing the questioning turned to Katie. "You have been mighty quiet young lady, do you have any problem with pretending that Grace was never a snake?" he asked.

Katie sat up straight, "I have no problem at all," she said, "I'd sooner that they blamed me. Grace is my best and most honest friend and she saved my life!"

40

MEETING THE D.A.

The next day a babysitter came to the Nelsons' house just before eight AM. The entire family, except the baby, would go to support Grace as she faced the police who were about to accuse her and Katie of a crime. It was an unusual gathering as the entire family knew Grace had committed the act of shifting into a snake and getting rid of Mr. Jennings. But because he could not stop abusing females, they all believed she was innocent, her behavior was not a crime. The distinction was clear as the family believed protecting oneself from further harm was the kids' right and took the criminality out of it. Still, if she had used a weapon, like a knife or a gun, there could be no equivocating about an actual homicidal act having occurred, but letting yourself react as a serpent would made it more natural.

If a gun or a knife had been used it would be sought, likely found, and called into evidence. In this case the police had sought the snake and found evidence of its existence with the slither marks and scales. In addition, the autopsy proving cause of death due to a poisonous snake bite confirmed that a snake was the "murderer" but they had no proof as to how the snake entered Jennings' apartment or even that the snake had not entered of its own accord. In defense of the girls, the lawyers were counting on the judge and or jury not being able to conceive of two little girls handling the poisonous snake. Yes, the snake was there, and probably the presence of the girls that same day could be proved, but they would argue that the one plus one did not equal three.

All of Grace's family were dressed in their best clothing as were Katie and Mrs. Jennings as they joined together; it was important to make a good impression to help support their credibility just on the off chance that someone could possibly think the girls capable of the hideous snake handling accusation. Once they were all seated in a meeting room the girls held hands. This was a very intimidating setting.

To enter the building, called a court house, they had to climb two sets of granite stairs separated from each other by a landing. Then at the top of those stairs was a wide bank of doors, but only one allowed you to pass into the building. These doors were massive in size and made of a dark stained oak with brass knobs and hardware. The other doors were locked and cordoned off by large velvet ropes fastened with brass clasps to brass stands keeping them about three feet in the air. This apparently helped ensure that everyone entered the court house via this central door through which they would be screened, pass their belongings through to be x-rayed, tested for COVID symptoms, and required to sign their names and state what their business was with the court.

Just getting into the building told the girls that this was a serious place and the rules would be followed. Then they were led to the meeting room which was made of the same dark oak with smoky looking windows on the corridor side and on the far side of the room huge widows banking to the outside. These windows were covered in bars so there would be no surprise escape from this room. It was a narrow room with a long table taking up most of its space. This table was surrounded by heavy wooden chairs, no cushions, a few had armrests. Both the table and chairs were made of the same dark stained oak, and the room was decorated with an American flag and photographs of retired judges at eye level; above the judges hung a photograph of the state governor and the seal of The State of Connecticut.

In keeping with the stark appearing furniture, the room was also very cool, much colder than the outside air. Grace and Katie were both thinking that this was about as scary as any building gets, maybe right up there with the dentist's office. They were wondering if they would even dare to talk in a place like this.

Their team all filtered into the room followed by the State's Attorney and the police who had been involved with this case. Most of them made eye contact with Grace and tipped their heads in greeting. No one shook hands anymore; even the police were respectful of COVID. The State's Attorney appeared to match the room and building in dignity and sternness. He was tall with a full head of white hair and wearing a dark suit. One small muscle near his left eye seemed to twitch on its own making Grace think that his entire being was under pressure and that was a valve. The expectations and intense fear could not have gotten any higher for the girls.

Then the State's Attorney began with a few opening remarks about why they were all there and the part each person could expect to play. When he got to Grace and Katie he seemed kindly, almost fatherly, saying that their job would simply be to tell the truth and allow the adults to sort out what had happened and what might need to be done about it. He went so far as to say that they had nothing to fear. Grace had been around enough trouble to know that this might be what this man hoped for, but not what she could count on. She looked at Katie and raised her eyebrows indicating "we'll see."

The story began to unfold, and Matt was on the spot for having lied to the police by saying he had stolen and delivered the snake when he had not. He apologized saying he had lost his cool out of fear that he somehow needed to protect his daughter that he should have known better, of course she had not been involved with a snake.

Then the emphasis went to Grace's strange DNA with both arachnid and viper markers unexplainable in a human being. Elena Maria said that there was a possible explanation in the fact that Grace had recently been bitten by both and had survived them. Her body must have made an adaptation of some kind in order to overcome the toxins. No research had ever been done to see how one might survive these bites if they were introduced close to each other. This research was too dangerous for human subjects and did not offer help to a broad enough sample of people to encourage such studies.

Finally the spotlight was on the children. Several neighbors of Mr. Jennings had seen the girls in disguises "hanging around" his apartment on the day in question. Further, an Uber driver had been called to pick up a boy and an old person needing a wheelchair, also on the day of the murder. Although he had admitted that he left them off several blocks away from the apartment in question, the description sounded most similar to the one the neighbors gave of the two kids in "disguise". It was hard to believe that there wasn't truth to these sightings.

Katie was prepared to confess what was true. She said they had dressed in costumes to go see her dad as they were hoping to perhaps harass him a bit by ringing on his bell and then pretending to be someone else, but they had decided he would see right through their disguises, so they had hung around a little trying to decide what to do and then they had just gone away.

"Just think," Katie said, "if we had actually rung his doorbell we might have been killed by the snake too! We were lucky to get away with our lives."

Grace was asked if she had anything to add and she shook her head "no" believing that the less she had to lie during this questioning the better off everyone would be.

But then Officer Winston stood up. He said, "If I may say a few words, there are some gaps in the information about how a snake may have entered the Jennings' apartment. In addition to this, when I went to question Grace recently I passed out cold, for quite a few minutes. I don't know what happened to me during that time, but I do have a vivid dream of having a snake come flying out from under the covers where I thought I would be seeing Grace. And I'm pretty sure it bit me, maybe even killed me but there is some weird force in that house, something that brought me back to life and made the snake disappear."

Grace looked stricken. Matt jumped to his feet saying "Now see here."

And the State's Attorney was totally perplexed by this weird and irregular testimony.

41

SWEET DREAMS AREN'T
MADE OF THESE

There was a timeout called in their meeting at the court house. Grace, Katie, their lawyers and families were asked to please step into the hallway. This area was like an echo chamber with cathedral height ceilings, a staircase that seemed to wind its way to heaven, and large dramatic inlays in the tile floor which must have been the State seal bearing words in Latin. The kids took it all in but didn't feel secure to even move six inches away from their parents. Everyone wondered what was going on back in the conference room where only the police who had worked on this case, the District Attorney, and an assistant remained. What could they possibly be debating? Grace imagined it was that she must be put on trial, for certainly she had committed some evil act on Mr. Jennings.

After what seemed like an hour, but was only twenty minutes, the door opened, and they were invited to return to their seats. Following a cue from the District Attorney, Officer Robert Winston stood and offered an apology to Grace and her family. He said that "studying the snakes and snake behavior had apparently disturbed me more than I had imagined. Since I slid around on the Jennings' apartment floor seeking clues I have been having dreams about snakes almost every night. In some of my dreams I was attacked by a whirling mass of snakes twisting around on each other and trying to ensnare me in their wriggling ball. I knew, in the dream, if that should happen I would be bitten and suffocated. On those occasions I woke up screaming and had to get up and drink a glass of bourbon before I could return to bed."

"On other nights I was reaching for Grace because I had found her fallen in a garden that resembled one on the side yard near her barn. As I knelt down to see if she was alright she would roll towards me, and what I would behold was a terrifically large snake baring its fangs and lunging at me. I would then jump backwards to escape her bite only to stumble and have her massive snake's body descend on top of me. We would wrestle; rolling, twisting, hissing and shouting until this dream was concluded with Grace, as a snake, sinking her fangs into my jugular. After that I would sleep as I was certain that I had just died."

The third scenario from his dreams was even more disturbing. "In this dream I was sent to kill Grace as she had the ability to turn at will into a hideous serpent. A pale and shaky Jennings had assigned me to put an end to Grace. His skin was slack and tinged with green, his eyes were dull yet penetrating, and he gave off the odor of death. He was the exact replica of the Jennings I had seen in the morgue and he came after me saying I must do my duty and protect the world from Grace. Jennings told me that Grace could be any snake she wanted to be or that she could shape shift into one of those Giant Goliath Bird Eating Spiders such as had nearly killed a man in her parents' basement a couple years back."

He went on to say that the Jennings' spirit knew that Bob, as he called him, had only joined the force to protect the public so this was his chance. He could protect every citizen from this monster, and he would become a well admired hero for detecting her deceptions and for being man enough to trap and defeat her. "This was the message," said Officer Winston, "that I was getting night after night. This is why I blurted out those thoughts against Grace. Of course she is a harmless child; of course no human can become a snake, of course she is innocent!"

With that, the State's Attorney thanked Officer Winston for his brave admissions of a somewhat personal nature, but which were necessary under these unusual circumstances. He also wanted to assure both the Nelson Family and the Jennings's that Officer Wilson would be taking some "well deserved" time off to catch up on some rest and also to seek a little counseling based on the traumatic nature of this case. He thought for now that no court date would be set, nor did he ever anticipate having to involve these children in the case again. The search for a snake in the wild, or for some snake keeper, would continue, but as far as he and his office were concerned this was a tragic accident of man losing against an unexpected attack by nature. Grace and Katie were free to go.

The two families stumbled out of the huge courthouse and into the light. The air was sweet and much of the day was wide open to them. They thanked their attorneys and shook hands trying not to seem as anxious to escape for East Apple as they were really feeling. There was peace to be found at home and security. For Grace the respite was one from all manner of influences from those who were dead and things that were beastlike. She no longer had a father who stepped back and forth in time but only one, flesh and blood dad who had proved that he loved her and who was loyal to her. She did not have to fear sudden and swift punishment from another world nor did she need to fear her own body playing tricks on her; tricks that might turn her into critters which even she could not control. She did not have to fear living while hiding lies from those she loved, nor did she have to pretend that her strange past did not exist for there were those who knew and still loved her. She had a dear mother, grandparents and even a best friend. She had a sense of sanity and freedom that she could not recall experiencing at anytime in her past.

Katie was equally happy. Although she had lost her dad recently, with his loss had come a sense of peace and freedom from torment, one which she could not enjoy while he was still alive to stalk and molest her. She too was thrilled to have the friendship with Grace and a happy home which included her mother and two siblings. She wanted to get back home and to start building happy memories that would put distance between her father's many abuses and the life of the girl she wanted to be and enjoy.

There was but one nagging fear which occasionally crossed Grace's mind, and that was would Officer Winston's therapy ever truly open up his memory? Might he be able to recall through some type of hypnosis or regressive therapy, although she did not know these terms, what had actually transpired in her bedroom on that day he had rushed up unattended and startled her as a snake? Would his actual reality ever reappear to interfere with her perfect new life? All she could do was to live her best life and to hope he felt better without having to remember if any of his dreams were actually based in reality.

Within a few days the two girls were enjoying a break from their worries and a break from their fears of COVID for the virus seemed under control, and their families were taking them for a long weekend to the beach in Rhode Island. Only Scruffy and Sybil would have to stay home with a caretaker. They were busily talking about what to pack and who could eat the most fried clams.

But a few miles away, Officer Robert Winston, newly on medical leave, was not involved in such fun. He woke up rather late in his own little house and, thanks to new medications, had slept pretty well. He still experienced some of the dreams, but they were not as horrific as they had usually been. Although the medication made him a bit groggy anything was better than being pursued by snakes.

He stumbled in and out of the bathroom then pushed the button to start his coffee and turned on the television for an all day news program as he had slept too late for the early morning news shows.

Much to his surprise some reporter was doing a show on the Jennings' case calling it an unsolved crime which their network would feature on the following Sunday evening. This reporter was doing what they called a 'tease' to promote the upcoming program. In this tease it was mentioned that much of the problem could likely be blamed on a bungling cop. Apparently an Officer Winston was fresh from police work on a college campus when he was assigned some detective duties for this homicide. The announcer appeared to both sneer at the police officer who had given him this assignment and at Officer Winston himself.

Bob was furious; he could feel his blood running cold with anger, and rage, how dare they besmirch his hard work and dedication. He decided to get dressed and go down and give that station and its managers a piece of his mind. He went into the bathroom to shave. He took up his razor and lifted his chin to begin slicing off his whiskers when he noticed an enormous thickening of his neck and a long, thin, spliced tongue darted out of his mouth flicking at his mirror image.

---The End---

REFERRAL INFORMATION

These are suggestions for help. School counselors, school nurses, and trusted adults will often assist with finding assistance.

1. Childhelp National Child Abuse Hotline
    1 – 800 422 4453
    Callers may remain anonymous
    The hotline is operated 24/7 and assistance offered in many languages

2. HAVOCA – Help for Adult Victims of Child Abuse
    havoca.org
    They will recommend therapists in callers' area, and support groups, but you must provide your name and contact information to receive.

3. National Association of Adult Survivors of Child Abuse
    www.NAASCA.org
    cell phones may use: naasca – mobile.org

Don't live alone with the pain.

ADDENDUM TO THE BOOK

https://www.amazon.com/dp/B097HTMVN2/ref=sr_1
_1dchild=1&keywords=AH%2CGRACE%21+by+
Cynthia&qid=1624036524&sr=8-1

If the reader will kindly go to the link above, click on the **stars** used to rate this book, and follow the directions your opinion of AH, GRACE! will be recorded and may help others interested in horror and suspense. It also helps the author. Many thanks, Cynthia H-B Adams

Made in the USA
Middletown, DE
27 June 2021